The word went out from Mars. *There are men in space again.*

Secretly and stealthily that word went out. Inward from Mars it traveled, across Earth and Venus and into the sun-bitten, frost-wracked valleys of Mercury. Outward from Mars it traveled, to the lunar colonies of Jupiter and Saturn. *There are men in space again.*

Human mind and muscle had challenged the dark robot ships and the Government suppression. The barriers that had been so strong were broken, the frontiers that had been closed were open, *The Lucy B. Davenport* became a symbol.

If she made it, she would have started the bright dreams once more. If she made it, she would end the absolute authority of the dark robot ships.

If she made it.

ALPHA CENTAURI
—OR DIE!

by
LEIGH BRACKETT

ace books
A Division of Charter Communications Inc.
A GROSSET & DUNLAP COMPANY
1120 Avenue of the Americas
New York, New York 10036

An ACE Book

There were no more men in space. The dark ships strode the ways between the worlds, lightless, silent, needing no human mind to guide them. The R-ships, carrying the freight and the passengers, keeping order, keeping the law, taking the *Pax Terrae* to the limits of the Solar System and guarding there the boundary which was not now ever to be crossed.

No more men in space. No strong hands bridling the rockets, no eyes looking outward to the stars. But still upon the wide-flung worlds of Sol were old men who remembered, and young men who could dream.

The shadow of the sandstone pillar lay black upon the ground. Kirby slipped into it and stood still, looking back the way he had just come. Wilson stopped too, in the shadow, asking nervously, "Nobody's following us, are they?"

Kirby shook his head. "I just wanted another look at the place. I don't know why, I've seen it often enough."

He had not been running. Neither he nor Wilson had been doing anything outwardly unusual, and yet Kirby was soaked with sweat and his heart was pounding. He could hear Wilson's heavy breathing, and he knew it was the same with him.

"I'm scared," said Wilson. "Why should I be scared now?" He was a young man, long and narrow, with very strong, very sensitive hands.

"The last time," Kirby said. "We only need a few more hours now, after all these years."

1

He let his voice trail off, as though he had been going to say more and decided not to, and Wilson muttered, "You're worried about March."

"He's been taking too much interest in my department lately. I wish I knew—"

"Yeah, Kirby, let's go."

"Take it easy. A minute more isn't going to matter."

The sandstone pillar, linked by chains to a line of other pillars, marked the westward limit of the section reserved for the fliers of spaceport personnel. Behind Kirby, three miles away, the great crystal dome of Kahora rose up from the desert, glowing splendidly with light. Under its protective shell the pastel city bloomed like a hothouse garden, bathed in warmed and sweetened air. Kahora was the Trade City for Mars, where the business of a planet was done in luxury and comfort.

Out here where Kirby stood the everlasting wind blew thin and dry across the wastes of half a world, edged with bitter dust, and the only light there was at hand came from the swift low moons. But the spaceport that served Kahora blazed with a white glare, and the control towers were tipped with crimson stars.

Kirby stood in the shadow and looked at this place where he had spent the years of his living burial since they barred the rockets from space. And now that he was through with it, now that he was never going to see it again, the hatred that he had for it could be let free. It was a long hate, and old hate. It had lived in him like a corrosive acid, poisoning everything he did or thought, poisoning the daytime and the nighttimes and even the times he spent

2

with Shari, which were the only good ones. He wanted to be rid of it.

Wilson muttered again about going, but Kirby didn't hear him. He was looking at the shops and sheds and multifarious buildings of the port, and in particular at the one called Parts and Supplies, which had been his personal prison. He was looking at the looming forest of towers that controlled the dark ships, that guided them back and forth between the worlds.

He was looking at the ships.

They lay in their massive cradles, ranged in rows according to type and size. The R-40 heavy freighters, the R-10 mixed carriers, the R-3 planetary patrol ships with the stings in their tails. Men worked over them. Cargo cranes rolled and rumbled, and the lights blazed. The ships lay, cold, lofty, soulless, enduring the probing of experts into their sensitive electronic brains because they must, but obedient to nothing and answering no master but the invisible impulses of beam and power.

Above all else, Kirby hated the ships.

He was older than Wilson. He could remember Kahora Post as it had been when the rockets roared and thundered across it. He could remember the barrooms that were around it, crowded with men from every world, speaking a thousand tongues. He could remember the spacemen's talk, and how some of them were already chafing at the barrier of Pluto's orbit, finding the System too small for them and looking hungrily at the stars beyond.

He could remember. He was a rocket man. He had seen every port in the System, or most of them, before he was twenty, and at twenty-six he had his master's ticket and was waiting for a ship. He had hated the dark robots then, because some day they were going to be a threat to trade. After their initial cost, a manned rocket could not compete with them. But that threat seemed a long way off.

He had his master's ticket, and presently he would have a ship, and by the time the robots got themselves established the way would be open to the stars and a whole new era would begin.

Kirby, hating in the shadow of the sandstone pillar, thought, "But it didn't happen that way. The new era never had a chance, because the old eras caught up to us first. The wars, the booms, the busts. One war, one bust too many."

And almost before anyone realized it, there were no more men in space.

Wilson shuffled his feet in the blowing dust. The stolen things were weighing heavy in his pockets, and he had still to face his wife. He said, "Let's go."

Kirby looked at the dark ships. "It was the planners that did it. The legislate-and-regulate, safety-and-security boys. From the cradle to the grave without one moment of personal risk. Well, they had what the people wanted right then, and maybe you can't blame them. They'd had a hard time of it. But—"

But damn them all eternally, even so. Because of them all the Stabilization Acts had passed. Trade Stabilization. Population Stabilization. Crop Stabilization. The busy minds of the experts working. Take the manned ships out of space and there can't be any trade wars or any other kinds of wars. The worlds can't get at each other to fight. Stop expansion outward to the stars and eliminate the risks, the economic upsets that attend every major change, the unpredictable rise and shift of power. Stabilize. Regulate. Control. We may lose a few unimportant liberties but think what we'll gain. Security for all, and for all time to come! And the dark ships of the Government will keep you safe.

"Inventories," said Kirby bitterly. "Do you know how many millions of inventories I've made out in that stinking Part's department?" Suddenly he laughed. "I wonder if they'll ever know how much I managed to hook out of those inventories?"

"Look," said Wilson. "Please. Let's get out of here."

Kirby shrugged and followed him. The fliers were not far away, small competent descendants of the helicopter, designed for family use like the old-fashioned automobile, and just as planet-bound. Wilson opened the door, but he didn't get in. A sudden reluctance seemed to have overtaken him.

"I thought you were in a hurry," Kirby said.

"Yeah. Damn it, Kirby, what am I going to tell her?"

"The truth."

"Oh, lord. She'll—I don't know what she'll do."

"All over Mars men are having the same trouble. Bull it through."

Wilson said sourly, "It's easy for you to talk."

"I've got my own troubles."

"I suppose so. But you have kids, Kirby. That's the thing. That's what she'll really blow her top about. And Kirby, you know, she's got a lot on her side."

"Listen, Wils. You knew you were going to have to do this from the beginning. It's tough on every-

5

body, but it's too late to back out now. You believe in what you're doing, don't you?"

"Sure. Yes. But—"

"Then go ahead. Some day your wife will come around to seeing that what you did was best."

Wilson said, "I hope I live that long." He climbed into his flier and slammed the door. Kirby stepped back. The rotors started to whir and then the small craft lifted straight up and skidded away toward the suburbs of Kahora. Kirby smiled crookedly and shook his head. He got into his own flier and took off. It ran smoothly by itself on autopilot, and he occupied his time by removing carefully from his pockets several dozen transistors he had just stolen from the government and placing them in a hidden compartment of his own designing.

By the time he was finished, the blazing dome of Kahora stood like a crystal wall on his left, showing through it a distorted vision of pastel buildings and gardens of many colors. Kirby glanced at it once, disinterested. It had always seemed to him a smothering place, where everything was soft and artificial, including the people. Like most of the resettled population, he lived outside the dome.

The suburbs were as pleasant as planning and effort could make them. Built long and low of the native clay, the houses suited the landscape and the cruel climate. Native desert growths filled out the dry gardens. They were not lovely, but they had an exotic charm of their own, much like the Earthly cactus and the Joshua tree. Kirby had not minded the place itself, only the law that required him to live there and forbade him to leave for any length of time this particular area of Mars.

The populations of the Solar System had been carefully figured to the last decimal point and portioned out among the planets according to food- and employment-potential, so that nowhere was there a scarcity or an overplus, and nobody's individual whim was allowed to upset the balance. If you wanted to change your residence from one sector or one world to another, the red tape involved was so enormous that men had been known to die of old age while waiting for a permit.

However, within the assigned sector you could move where you wanted to, and so almost the whole population of the suburban settlement worked and schemed and sweated and toiled to get inside the dome. It was a status symbol, a matter of prestige, even more than it was a matter of the undeniably greater comfort. With some it became an obsession. Kirby remembered that when his wife had succumbed to a mutant virus that swept the colony, his first feeling had been relief that he would no longer have to hear about Kahora.

If she had lived, he thought, this would have been easy. I wouldn't even have said good-bye. But now there is Shari, and that makes it not easy.

He remembered what he had said to Wilson. Be brave and bull it through, make her come whether she wants to or not. Good, stern, sensible advice. Only he himself was not going to take it, and Wilson had known he was not going to take it. He felt cowardly and ashamed, thinking of the men all over Mars who were going through the same ordeal as Wilson, trying to explain their patent lunacy to shocked and irate wives. And he was not going to say a word to Shari. Not even, out loud, good-bye.

The flier passed over the streets of the suburb where he had lived once, long ago, but he did not see them. There was a low ridge beyond the suburb, and on the other side was the Martian town, the very ancient town that had been the original Kahora, and as great a city in its day as the new one was now. From the air one could see how shrunken it was, with wide abandoned fringes that crumbled slowly away into nothingness. The ruins of the King City, the old battlemented stronghold of the rulers, stood up dark and lonely against the racing moons, and at its battered feet there curved the deep-gouged bed of a navigable river, dry and choked with dust.

Kirby set his flier down beside a flat-roofed house on a winding street. He went inside. And she was waiting for him.

He had never come home in all these years that she had not been waiting for him, no matter what the hour, and almost always she was smiling. Tonight she was not smiling. Tonight she was not as she had ever been before, and her eyes, the color of smoky topaz set a little obliquely in a high-boned face, held a look that he had never seen, a look that did not come into the eyes of the Earth women, a fey look, wild and sombre. It made Kirby shiver. He started to speak, to ask her the reason for her strangeness, but she came to him swiftly and said, in the old High Martian,

"Beloved, there is danger, close behind you."

Kirby's heart began to pound again. He reached out and caught her, almost roughly, her strong slim shoulder under his hand. "Danger, Shari? What do

8

you mean, danger?" She was not even dressed in her customary way. She wore a coverall and boots, as though she might be planning a long trip into the desert. "What's all this? What are you—"

"I'm going with you," she said.

Kirby had told her nothing. No single word had ever been said between them. "Going with me?" he said, and stared at her, not believing. "You're talking nonsense. What's the matter with you?"

"You weren't even going to say good-bye." Now she smiled, and shook her head.

Kirby was alarmed. "Who's been talking to you, Shari?"

"I am Martian, Kirby. I have no need for talk."

He thought he understood what she meant, and her eyes frightened him with the wisdom that was in them. He turned away and said desperately, "You don't know where I'm going. You don't know what the chances are, you don't realize—"

"You are going a great distance, Kirby. Farther than men have ever gone before. I know. And if you were going farther still, I would go with you."

She had a bundle packed. He saw it, neatly rolled and tied with cords, and it was a small thing, not much to carry away into the dark beyond. He looked around suddenly at the room he knew so well, the beautiful ancient things, the priceless carpet worn thin as silk but nothing of its brightness lost, the wide couch and the low tables carved from woods that had not grown on Mars for millenia, the little familiar things. He said, "How long have you lived in this house, you and your family before you?"

She smiled. "What is time on Mars? Besides, I'm

9

the last. What matter if I lose this now or in a little while?" She put something into his hand. "Here is a gun, Kirby. You will have to use it."

He stared at the unfamiliar thing, unfamiliar because it was so many years since he had seen one, and then he looked at her sharply. "You were talking about danger."

She nodded to the window place, where the shutters were open to the moonlight. "Listen, and you will hear it coming."

II

There was a thrumming in the sky.

"Fliers," Kirby said. "Two of them."

Shari picked up her bundle. "We can be away in yours before they reach here."

"No. They'd have us smack on their radarscopes, and I don't dare lead them—"

He did not finish what he was about to say. Instead he shoved the gun out of sight under his loose shirt and grabbed Shari's bundle. "Peel off that coverall," he said. "Quick."

There were cushions and bright silks on the couch. He hid the bundle among them and sprawled out on top of it, a man at ease, a man without a care in the world. Shari's ugly garment vanished also among the silks. By the time the fliers droned down to a landing outside she looked as she always did, a skirt-like wrapping of pale green girdled around her hips,

10

her breasts bare after the Martian fashion, with a collar of hammered metal plaques above them.

"Fix us a drink," said Kirby.

She bent over a low table and said softly, "These men are from the Port, with your brother that is not of the blood but of the law."

"March," said Kirby, and his eyes narrowed. He moved on the cushions, feeling the hard comforting pressure of the gun against his flesh. Then he asked Shari, "Have you always had this . . . gift?" He tapped his forehead. "I mean, all these years you could read my mind, and I never knew it?"

He was glad that all his thoughts about her had been good ones.

She almost laughed at him. "I never used it—well, hardly ever, really—except to tell me when you were coming. A Martian man could guard his mind, but not you, so it would not have been fair. And I never told you of it because it might have made you uncomfortable."

Kirby shook his head in awe. "A telepath. I'll be damned. I knew Martians were supposed to have some unusual abilities, but I never dreamed—"

"Not all of us, Kirby, and the effort is too great to waste it on trivialities. Already my head aches." She put the tall glass in his hand and then she kissed him briefly, fiercely, and whispered, "Be careful! And now I'll let them in."

The knocking on the door had just begun. Shari opened it, and three men came in. Two of them were government agents assigned to Port Security, and Kirby reckoned that there must be two more outside, searching his own flier. The third man was his

11

brother-in-law, Harry March. He was also Divisional Superintendent and Kirby's superior.

Kirby sat up. "I won't say welcome, Harry, because you're not." He looked at the government men. "What is this?"

March glanced slowly around the room, letting his gaze slide over Shari as though she were not there. He was a tall man. He had never been muscular, and though he was not fat there were paddings of soft flesh on his cheeks and belly. His features were narrow and pronounced, very like the features of Kirby's dead wife, and his attitude was as hers had been, one of deep disapproval of practically everything. He had never, since Kirby's remarriage, visited him at home.

Kirby asked, "What did you have to say that couldn't be said during working hours?"

Flatly, with only the faintest undertone of satisfaction, March said, "You're under arrest."

Kirby sprang up. "Listen, Harry, a citizen still has some rights under this fine benevolent government. You can't just walk in—"

One of the government men stepped forward, pulling a paper out of his pocket. "Warrant," he said. "You're charged with a long lot of words, but it boils down to theft of government property, corruption of government employees, and suspicion of sabotage. That enough for you?"

"I guess so," said Kirby, "except that Harry is crazy if he thinks he can pin it on me. Where's your evidence, Harry? You can't put me in prison just because you hate my guts." Kirby was astounded at the sound of his own voice, honest and angry and not the least bit frightened. Inside he was quaking, and cold as ice.

March said quietly, "I have what evidence I need. But the thefts are not the important part, Kirby. It's what you're doing with the things. There's no market for them, you can't sell them anywhere—there must be another reason. I have a good idea what it is, but I want you to tell me."

"You do," said Kirby, and smiled.

March's thin mouth grew thinner. "I know what you're up to, whether you tell me or not, and you know what the penalty is." He came forward a little. "I'm trying to help you, not for your sake but because you were my sister's husband, and I don't want her name involved in criminal proceedings. If you'll make a full confession now, with the names of all other persons connected with this business, I'll withdraw my charges against you. I'll even go so far as to say that you were acting for me."

Kirby glanced at the two government men. "And what would they say?"

"They'll go along with me."

The government men nodded. Kirby laughed. "That important, is it? Well, I'm sorry, Harry. This is the only chance you've ever had to be a hero, and I'm going to louse it up. I don't know anything. I don't even know what you're talking about."

The two men who had remained outside to search Kirby's flier came in. One of tthem shook his head and said, "Nothing in it." Kirby took a long drink from the glass he still held in his hand and put it down. "Harry," he said, "don't you think you're letting your dislike for me carry you just a little too

13

far?" He nodded at the government men. "Wasting their time, on a personal feud."

"There's no feud," March said. "For your own good, Kirby, I'm asking you to talk."

"Oh, but there is a feud," said Kirby, moving a little to the right. "There always was, right from the first. You thought your sister was much too good for me. You know something, Harry? Your sister was a mess, and why I didn't see it in time I'll never know. She was selfish and hen-brained and trouble-making, and Mars has been a better place since she left it." Underneath his words his mind was signalling frantically to Shari. "Now! Now! Can you do something to distract them?" It seemed a lunatic thing to depend on telepathy, but it was all he had.

March was genuinely shocked. He stared at Kirby for a moment, and then his face began to darken. He said, "You have no right to speak that way." He looked at Shari. "Especially after—" He had to try twice to get the words out. "A native woman!"

"That'll be enough of that, Harry," Kirby said very quietly.

March turned to the government men. "He's going to be stubborn and we can't afford stubbornness now. Even a few hours of stalling on Kirby's part might be enough to let the ship take off without him."

Kirby's nerves contracted with a stabbing pain. It was no surprise to him that March had guessed the truth, but he hated to hear the bald flat mention of a thing that had been so well and lovingly hidden for so long. Shari said softly, in the ceremonial High Martian that few Earthmen understood, "It is only a guess. And now I am going to speak."

14

One of the government men got out a flat case with a syringe in it. "I figured we'd have to use this," he said laconically, and Kirby shivered. The truth-drugs developed since the days of scopolamine were very good. Too good. They worked.

Why the hell didn't Shari do something?

She did. She spoke suddenly and clearly in English, which she knew perfectly but almost never used. She spoke to March, and her eyes were fixed on his with that queer, fey look that seemed to strip his mind down naked. Kirby saw him trying to turn away from it, but he could not. It held him fascinated. And Shari said, "It is not because of your dead sister that you hate Kirby. You hate him because he is a man, and you are not."

A curious change came over March's face, slight at first, so slight that Kirby hardly noticed it. Shari's clear relentless voice went on.

"You cannot understand love or friendship. You hate courage because you have none yourself. You are eaten up with hatred and poisoned with envy, but you are not even wicked. You are nothing."

March said, in a strange subdued voice, "Hold your tongue." And he added a Low Martian word that every Earthman knew if he knew no other.

Shari laughed. "The men you work with have a word for you, March. Shall I tell you what it is?"

She looked now at the government men, who became suddenly flushed and uneasy. One of them started to say something, and at the same time March gave back a step and turned, and another of the men snickered. March winced, drawing back his lips in the grimace of a child about to cry. Kirby could not bear to look at him. He had always had a

15

healthy detestation for his brother-in-law, but this was abominable and he wished Shari had not done it.

Then the reason for her doing it came back to him, and he pulled the gun from underneath his shirt. No one noticed. They were all occupied with March and Shari.

"All right," he said. "Everybody stand still. Get your hands up."

Immediately he was the center of attention. For a second or two nobody did move. They were stricken with astonishment at the sight of a gun. They had never dreamed that he might be armed. Nobody was armed any more. It was unheard of. Even the government police carried only shockers that stunned but did not kill. Kirby was grateful to whatever male relative of Shari's it had been who buried this forbidden relic of the bad old days in the Martian city of Kahora.

"It shoots bullets," he said, so they should all understand. "It was built to be lethal, not polite, and my marksmanship is very rusty. I couldn't guarantee just to cripple you. Starting one by one from the left, will you move away from the door? Shari, close the shutters."

Uncertainly, looking at each other as men do who are momentarily at a loss and hoping for an example from somebody else, March and the government men began to move. Kirby heard the shutters bang, and then Shari came up beside him. The man with the drug case was still holding it in his upraised hand Kirby said, "You. Let it drop."

Shari cried, "He'll throw it!"

Kirby ducked. The hard case flashed past hi

head. The man reached fast for the shocker that was holstered under his armpit. Kirby fired. The gun made a very loud noise. The man doubled up and sat down on the floor. Kirby saw movement among the others. He fired again, and missed, but the bullet whined close between two heads, and the movement stopped. March had turned an ashen gray. He leaned against the wall, not saying anything, waiting to be sick. Kirby did not feel so well himself. He kept glancing at the man who was rocking back and forth over his knees and sobbing.

"He is not dying," Shari said, answering his thought. "It is only that he does not care for pain. Keep them still while I bind them."

They were ready to be still now. Shari laughed. "They do not love the government enough to die for it. They are all thinking that they have done their best, and now it is up to others." Her hands worked swiftly. Suddenly she stopped. "Kirby, they are thinking that the R-ships will track you down and destroy you and all the others."

"Go ahead, tie them up." Kirby went and stuck the muzzle of the gun close to March's face. "Have the R-3's been alerted?"

"Yes. You can't escape them, Kirby. They'll find your ship, they'll smash it up, they'll smash you and all the others, and there won't be any mercy."

He was screaming like a woman. Kirby hit him across the mouth, not out of vengefulness but to stop the ugly noise. Shari said quietly, "He lies. It is done now, Kirby. Come."

She found her bundle and her coverall, bunching them together under her arm. Kirby went with her out the door, shutting it carefully behind them. The shots had not attracted any crowd. He had not thought they would. The Martians had a way of letting Earthmen handle their own troubles without interference.

Kirby walked fast toward the fliers. "What about the R-3's, Shari? Could you read his mind?"

"The authorities are waiting at the port. They thought there would be no trouble about handling you, but they knew that it might take a little time if the drugs had to be used. They know you're here, of course; March told them when he landed."

"Yeah. We have some leeway, then?"

"Until at the port they begin to wonder why no further report has been made." She put her hand to her head and pressed it. "I wish I were better at this. My brain is cracking open."

Kirby hesitated, looking at the three craft and scowling. Then he thrust Shari into his own and said, "I'll be back in a second. Maybe I can stall 'em a while longer."

His own communicator would not operate on the official UHF band, which was closed to civilians. He climbed into one of the other fliers and bent over the radio. Then he hesitated again, overcome by a prudent desire to let well enough alone. For precious seconds he stood there fingering the switch, trying to make up his mind. "Bull by the horns," he muttered at last. He was afraid of the R-3's. Any risk was worthwhile if it held them back a little longer. He began to search his pockets. "Damn it, I never have a handkerchief. Oh, well, this'll do." He hauled out his shirttail and wrapped it over his mouth. Then he opened the switch and spoke, pitching his voice

18

a bit high. "Port Security. This is March, calling Port."

"Receiving you. What's going on?"

Kirby's voice cracked from sheer nervousness, giving an impression of excitement he could not have counterfeited. "Everything's fine. Kirby put up more resistance than we looked for, but he's under the drugs now and as soon as they take effect we'll have the whole story."

"Good. Any trouble with the woman? We don't want to get involved with the Martian authorities."

"No trouble," Kirby said. "I'm going back in the house now. I don't want to miss anything. We'll keep you posted."

"Right. Remember, we want the information as soon as you get it. We're ready to act the minute we have anything to go on."

Kirby mumbled something about patience and it wouldn't be long now. Port Security signed off. Kirby closed the switch, remembering some big stones that lay on the ground outside. He got one and went to work with it, in a violent hurry. When he was through both official communicators and both flight control panels were out of commission. If March and the others should get free it would not do them any immediate good.

Shari was waiting quietly. She said nothing while he lifted off and sent his flier rushing at full power along an oblique course that led out over the desert. She seemed very tired, and there were lines of pain around her mouth. Kirby leaned over and kissed her.

"You can rest now. You've saved us time."

She shook her head and sighed. "I'll have to. My mind is tired. Until I've slept it will be useless."

With more control over her nerves that Kirby could have mustered, she slid down in the padded seat and slept, almost at once. He looked at her. Since the decision had been hers, unsought and unsuggested, he was glad she had come. She was too much a part of him to be left behind now, and there was another reason, too. The whole venture had shifted abruptly into a sharper focus. He was savagely determined that it had to succeed, all the way, because nothing must happen to Shari.

The desert reeled away beneath them, mile on empty mile, with nothing to break its desolation but an occasional wandering dust-devil. The moons sank out of sight. Once Kirby saw in the distance the black line of a canal with a town beside it, pricked out with a scattering of torches. The Earthman's civilization did not reach this far into the heart of Mars. There was only timelessness and a long slow dying. The stars burned magnificently overhead in the thin dry air. Kirby studied them with a kind of intimacy. He was afraid, and yet he felt as he had not felt in years, not since he was a green kid stepping away from Earth for the first time, outbound for strange new worlds.

He pushed the flier to the limit of its speed, and it was fast, but there was not time enough given to him. He had still a long way to go when the Urgent signal shrilled from his communicator. A second or two later a man's harsh voice called out his own name, and added, "Acknowledge at once!"

Kirby did not acknowledge. There was nothing he wanted to say, and he was not going to oblige

20

them with a carrier wave so they could fix his position. He waited.

"This is your last warning, Kirby. Your only chance is to obey instructions immediately. The R-3's have been sent out."

III

Shari had wakened. She straightened up and looked at Kirby. "Shall we be able to make it?"

"I don't know. Depends on how long it takes the R-3's to locate us. They'll have to hunt, and there's a lot of desert around Kahora. On the other hand, they're fast. A hell of a lot faster than we are."

He looked around apprehensively, but there was no sign of anything yet in the sky, nor did his radarscope show any warning pip. Shari put her hand over on top of his.

"I think perhaps luck will be with us," she said. "You're afraid now, but it is mostly for me. Don't be. Whatever happens, it could not have been any other way."

He took her hand and squeezed it savagely. "I'll see to it nothing does happen. Damn it, this desert always did seem to go on forever. Won't those blasted mountains ever show?"

It seemed to Kirby that the flier barely moved. His heart thumped painfully, and every nerve-end was awake and leaping. He hunched over the controls, trying to urge the small craft forward as one does a horse, with his own body. And then Shari said a surprising thing. She said, "For the first time since I have known, you are happy."

"Happy!" he said. He laughed.

"But you are. I think it's because for the first time you feel free. The net is broken. You may die, but you will not again be a prisoner."

He grunted. "I wouldn't know. Right now I don't feel anything at all but scared."

Ahead of him, out of the gloom, there lifted a jagged wall, not high, because the ceaseless tramping of the centuries had worn away the soil, and then the softer rock, and then the hard rock, grinding them into powdery dust to roll away with the wind, so that only a rag and bone of a mountain chain was left. But it was the thing Kirby was looking for. He shouted suddenly, and on the heels of his exuberance, like a jeering echo, came the first monotonous peet-peet-peet from the radarscope, and a bright little pip showed up at the edge of the screen.

"The mountains are close," said Shari.

"So is the R-3. And look at it come!"

The bright pip moved like a shooting star across the screen. The intensity of the single note increased rapidly. Kirby groaned. The gnawed and ancient peaks were not ahead of him now, but underneath, and the place he wanted to get to was so agonizingly near at hand.

His communicator clamored at him suddenly. It was the port Control Center, where the men with the dials and the indicators and the screens and the infinite numbers of gadgets controlled the R-ships, guiding them, receiving a constant stream of data from them, making the decisions and the final pushings of the ultimate buttons.

"You're centered, Kirby. You have ten seconds before the proximity trip releases the first missile—unless we stop it. You're being given one more chance. Acknowledge!"

The voice began to count, down.

Kirby glanced aside at Shari. Then he reached out fast and clicked over the switch. "Kirby acknowledging! This is Kirby—hold your fire!"

"All right." The voice sounded relieved. "Now listen carefully. Here's the deal. We want the starship, and we want it now, right away, fast. We know you're close to it. Lead on, and we'll use that missile on it instead of on you."

"What happens to me afterward?" asked Kirby sullenly.

"You'll be alive. So will the person you have with you. You haven't anything to lose. And you know we'll get the starship anyway."

"Then why make deals with me?"

"We'd rather get it on the ground, before there's even an attempt at taking off. Psychological reasons."

Kirby glared at the passing peaks beneath him, lines drawn deep between his brows. At last he said heavily, "It's in the cleft of the sea bottom, about seventy miles ahead."

"Good. We thought you'd see reason. As soon as the R-3 picks it up visually we'll notify you to turn around and come home."

"All right." Kirby's voice rose to a sharper edge. "I just want you to know that I'm not giving up for myself. I'd just as soon get blown to hell as live like a sheep any longer. But you're right, I've got somebody with me. My wife."

"It all adds up to the same thing. Go ahead,

Kirby, but be very careful. That proximity trip is all ready to go the minute anything looks wrong."

"Don't get impatient," Kirby snarled. "I'm right on course. Seventy miles."

"We're patient people. And leave your communicator open."

Kirby turned to Shari. She was leaning toward him, toward the microphone. Her eyes were very bright. Abruptly, in a shrill loud tone that was not like her usual voice at all, she began to upbraid him, calling him a coward, a weakling, an old woman, and going on from there in Low Martian to language he would not have thought she knew. He answered her back, irritably at first and then more and more angrily, until they were shouting at each other and the narrow confines of the cabin rang with it. Faintly from the speaker Kirby could hear the man at Control Center laughing.

Moving as silently as he could he slid out of the seat and opened his secret hiding place and shifted the precious transistors into his pockets. The night beyond the cabin windows showed intensely dark. Shari's voice pealed on, rising to a fishwifely frenzy. He roared back at her, using out of three vocabularies every dirty word he could lay his tongue to, and handed her her rolled-up bundle. Then he reached over and shoved a lever on the panel.

The flier lurched. A volley of deafening explosions broke out and the starboard wing rotor went crazy. Shari screamed, "Do something, you fool, you idiot! We're going to crash!"

Kirby yelled into the microphone, "Hold back your damned robot, I've got to slow down!"

"What's wrong?"

"Are you deaf or something? I've been pushing this crate too hard and she's hot and she's jammed." Kirby fought the controls grinning, the sweat pouring down his face. He nodded to Shari. Under cover of the racket the motor was making she opened the cockpit door, never once pausing in her maniacal shrieks.

"I'm slowing down," Kirby told Control Center. "Don't run over me. Damn you, Shari, shut up!" He brought his palms together with a hard cracking sound. She let out one last yip and was quiet, crouching by the open door, the wind whipping her silken skirt around her legs.

Control Center said, "We're synchronizing speed. Can you clear your motor?"

Kirby worked the lever. The motor choked, roared for a minute into life, and then choked again. There were further explosions. He throttled down some more and made another adjustment. The motor coughed and began to chug along quite normally.

Kirby said, "Yeah. But I'll have to take it easy and let her cool. There's no hurry anyway."

The worn eroded heap of mountain below was gashed with shallow valleys, welling now with darkness. Kirby had lost altitude along with speed. The ridges and plateaus that walled the valleys in were not too far below, not much farther than a man could jump if he wasn't afraid to take a chance.

"Listen, Kirby," said the voice from Control Center grimly, "if that ship takes off before we reach it, the deal's no good. You understand that."

"They won't take off without me, not if they can help it."

"Why are you so important?"

"You don't realize what a rare commodity I am."
Kirby was very still now, very tense. His eyes moved
sharply from the instrument panel to the black night
ahead, and then back again. The flier was going by
itself now on autopilot. His right hand was raised,
and Shari watched it, crouching by the open door.
Kirby said to the microphone, "In this day and age,
an experienced spaceman with a master's raging
who's still young enough to move without creaking
is worth his weight in diamonds to the right people.
You bet I'm important."

A dim plateau slid out of the darkness, close underneath. Kirby counted under his breath, and then
his upraised hand flashed down. Before the gesture
was finished, Shari jumped.

"Is that why you got into this, Kirby? To be important, to be a spaceman again?"

"Oh, hell," said Kirby, "what difference does it
make now? All I wind up being is a Judas goat, and
inside of an hour the ship will be a pile of junk. Just
be content with what you've got and don't worry
about motives." He made a dial setting on the autopilot. "Another five minutes and I can increase speed
again, if that'll make you any happier."

"Kirby—"

"Oh, shut up. This is bad enough without having
to yak about it."

"Okay. If that's the way you want it."

Silence.

Kirby rose and crept to the door and jumped.

He had waited almost too long. The plateau was
not wide, and he hit so close to the drop-off that he
thought he was going to go over. He lay flat on the
rock, jarred to the marrow by the fall, and watched

his flier buzzing purposefully away on its course. The small plateau was the last jug of the mountains. Here they fell away into a great deep gulf that had held an inland sea as big as the Caspian, in the days before Mars began to die.

He lay still, watching, and presently above him a shadow passed.

It passed without a sound, not twenty feet over his head, as a shark passes over a swimmer in deep water, unhurried, huge, and potent with a devouring fury. The starlight touched its tapering flanks with a cold pale glimmer and brought to the lensed "eyes" on its forward surface an eerie glint of life. Kirby knew that those eyes were no more than electric cameras, and that they were blinded by the dark. When they needed to "see" the powerful floodlights would click on and give them day, but they were not looking for anything yet. Even so, he shrank closer to the rock, fighting off a horrid conviction that this unnatural child of the guided missile and the pilotless plane was a living thing, sentient, all powerful, and eager to slay.

It passed on, leaving only a whisper of air behind it, following the flier. It pleased Kirby to think of the very small robot innocently betraying its savage cousin. He got up off the rock, calling for Shari, and a man's voice spoke to him out of the darkness.

"Kirby! Kirby, is that you?"

"Yeah." He made out a nervous shadow and went toward it, recognizing it as Hockley, a power-installation technician from a secondary spaceport over on the other side of Mars. Hockley was crouching beside a heap of carefully arranged stones that concealed a field telephone, permanent equipment on

27

this lookout post, and somebody was talking over the phone in a way that verged on the hysterical. But Hockley was paying no attention to it. He was staring after the dark ship.

Kirby took the phone. He spoke into it briefly, giving the exact coordinates of the course being taken by the flier and the R-3. Then he said, "Is everybody accounted for?"

The voice on the other end said, "Now that you're here. You're late."

"Get 'em all strapped in. We're coming down."

"Make it fast."

Kirby put the phone away and shouted again for Shari. She had come up quietly while he talked and was standing beside him, waiting. They started off, the three of them, down the broken, tumpled path that twisted to the foot of the long slope. Both men had made the trip many times before. Sliding and skidding on the steep stretches, raising a trail of fine dust, they went down the drop at a speed that was not quite reckless, alternately helping Shari. On both sides of the path there stretched curious mounds and heaps of stone, a few of them still betraying a rectangular shape. Shari said abruptly, "This was once a city."

Kirby nodded. "It was a port, until the sea dried up and left it." He stopped suddenly, digging his heels in the dust. Out over the sea bottom a tiny nova had burst and died.

"That," said Kirby, "was my flier. Control Center is not so dumb as I had hoped."

Hockley said something between a curse and a prayer. "It'll come back now, looking for us."

A shaft of light, distant but blinding bright, ap

peared like a pillar upon the desert. It moved. Hockley groaned and flung himself on along the path. Kirby was right on his heels.

They passed the harbor quays, huge broken monoliths worn round and shapeless, still lying dutifully along the edges of a deep gorge that had once been filled with blue water but was now only a naked gash in the rock. There was a way down the cliff, a way like a broad stair. Men had made it, men following the shrinking sea. Fishermen and traders, climbing down to their boats. The mouths of great caverns on both sides of the way, holes gnawed out of the cliff in ages gone by the action of the water. The two men and the woman ran, their feet clattering on the stone. The bright pillar moved swiftly over the sea bottom, light for the R-3's searching eyes.

In the darkness on the floor of the dry harbor there was hurried movement and a sound of voices, and a glinting of the cold stars off colder metal. The mobile-launch interceptor missile they were readying down there was not very much larger than a child's toy, but even in that dim light one would know instantly that it was nothing to play with.

Hockley said, "I wish we had more of those. I wish we had a thousand."

"One ought to be enough."

There was a flash, a hiss, and a nerve-chilling whine that vanished away almost before it was heard. Kirby stopped running, holding tight to Shari's hand. Hockley stopped. They stood motionless. Seconds crawled by like years, and nothing happened. Hockley whispered, "They missed."

"They couldn't. They had the course. Besides,

those babies find their own targets, that's what they're built for."

A second nova, vastly larger, flared and fell, and after an interval came the shock-wave and the noise. Kirby laughed.

"Control Center wasn't expecting that. Now we go!"

They half fell the rest of the short way to the bottom. A little group of men received them. The portable rack from which they had launched the missile had already been shoved aside, out of the way. All together they plunged into a vast lopsided opening in the cliff as high as two cathedrals. There were lights in there, carefully shaded so that no gleam reached outside. There were numerous fliers, parked together in a bay of the cavern. Around the walls there were forges and machine tools, collected painfully piece by piece over the years, patched together, cannibalized, improvised and jury-rigged with the utmost ingenuity. There was the litter of much working.

And there was a ship.

Shari uttered a small cry of surprise. "But it's so ugly!"

"What did you expect?" snapped Kirby. "For an ex-tramp freighter—"

She laughed. "I'm sorry. But in your mind its image has been clothed with such beauty!"

They stumbled up the gangplank, crowding the narrow lock that had over its inner door in faded letters, "LUCY B. DAVENPORT, TERRA."

Inside there was pandemonium. Men were shouting. An uproar of women's voices filled all the spaces within the hull, punctuated by the bawlings of children. The outer door of the lock clanged shut. Kirby gave Shari's hand a final squeeze and left her to shift for herself. He too began to shout, running forward along the corridor. Somebody heard him and got hold of the intercom, ordering everyone to shut up and prepare for take-off. Nobody seemed to pay much attention. It still sounded to Kirby like riots going on all over the ship. He clattered up the ladder into the bridge and slammed the door behind him. It was quieter. "Get the hell out of there, Pop," he said to the old man who was sitting in the pilot's chair.

Pop Barstow grinned at him. "I was hoping you wouldn't show up, so's I could take the old Ark off myself." He slid into the co-pilot's place and laid the webbing over his lank middle.

Kirby said grimly, "You may get your chance yet. Give 'em the siren."

He punched the firing keys. A great roaring filled the cavern and the deck beneath him leaped. The siren began to wail. The ship's bow-light came on, outlining the cavern's mouth in a hard white brilliance. Sitting stiff and quivering in the pilot's chair, Kirby began to nurse the *Lucy B. Davenport* forward along the launchway that had been prepared for her. It had been a long time since he held a ship under his hands. Too long. He was scared. Maybe he couldn't do it any more. Maybe he'd crash her, with all those screaming women and kids. With Shari.

"Butterflies?" asked Barstow.

Kirby shook his head. "Buzzards."

"You're too young, Kirby. Let me have her."

Kirby laughed. They were clear of the cavern now

31

—almost. A little bit farther. His insides felt as
though they were caught in a vise. They hurt.

Shaw, the radarman, said suddenly, "I'm picking
up something." From the back of the bridgeroom
where he bent over the 'scope there came the monotonous, nerve-clawing bleat of the signal, still faint
but growing louder.

"More R-3's," said Barstow. "Well, young Kirby,
are you going to let 'em catch us?"

They were clear of the cavern. Kirby shut his jaws
together and leaned forward over the control bank.
The belly jets cut in with a howl and a burst of
flame. The ship rose up enormously as though on a
column of fire, and the stern jets opened wide to full
power. The *Lucy B. Davenport* pointed her nose to
the black sky and went up screaming, leaving behind her a roll of apocalyptic thunder. Almost before Kirby knew it they were in silence and open
space, and the radarscope was blank.

Pop Barstow reached solemnly inside his shirt and
came out with a bottle. He drank and passed it to
Kirby, who needed it.

"Well," said Barstow, "so far, so good. We made
it."

Kirby gasped and ran his hand over his mouth,
passing the bottle back. He looked out through the
bow port. The landing light was off, and there was
space, where he had lived once until he was pri-
soned on a planet. It had not changed. The stars
burned just as bright, and the gulfs between them
were as deep and dark and cold. He shivered, a
shallow twitching of the skin. He was a stranger
here now, an intruder. Space no longer belonged to

a man. It was the kingdom of the dark ships, of which the R-3's had been only the small foretaste.

At her present desperate rate of acceleration, the *Lucy B. Davenport* would be clear of the System and beyond the range of the interplanetary control stations before even the Mars-based ships could catch her. They had timed their takeoff very carefully for that. From then on there was nothing between them and their destination but space—4.3 light-years of it.

But even in the immensity of interstellar space, there was no safety. Here, too, the dark ships had outstripped man. And it was only a question of time.

"Yeah," said Kirby heavily, "we made it. Now all we have to do is wait, and wonder every second if the R-ships can run us down."

IV

The word went out from Mars. *There are men in space again.*

Secretly and stealthily that word went, on the tight Government beams. But it was heard and repeated. Inward from Mars it traveled, across Earth and Venus and into the sun-bitten, frost-wracked valleys of Mercury. Outward from Mars it traveled, to the lunar colonies of Jupiter and Saturn, to the nighted mining camps of the worlds beyond. *There are men in space again!*

Human mind and muscle had challenged the dark

ships, and the barriers that had been so strong were broken, the frontiers that had been closed were open, and a thing had been done so splendid and insane and terrifying that it struck the mass consciousness with the impact of a bomb. There was no longer any point in feigning secrecy. The news services broadcast the story, training expressive cameras on the comfortable houses left vacant and forlorn, the abandoned toys, the supper dishes untouched on dusty tables.

Neighbor women shook their heads for a System-wide audience, lamenting the tragic fate of those whose husbands and fathers had so forcibly betrayed them. Two prospective passengers who had fled screaming into the night, leaving their husbands to go starward alone, gave solemn interviews and received much sympathetic attention. To that portion of the population given to feeling intensely about things, the *Lucy B. Davenport* became a symbol.

To most she was the black shadow of reaction, the last resurgence of the bad old days. But to some, chiefly the boys and the young men with the dreams not quite stamped on them yet, she was the bright single spark in a dreary monotone of settled routine. If she made it, she would have started something.

If she made it, she would have ended something, too—the absolute authority of the dark ships.

If she made it.

Here and there, scattered through the Solar System, certain men—other Kirbys and Wilsons and Barstows—had a special interest in the outcome. The *Lucy B. Davenport* was not only the only survivor of the Age of Rockets, cherished in the secrecy of waste places. It was not possible that she should

34

have been. The law requiring the surrender and destruction of all manned ships was a challenge to the rebellious old Adam inherent in the human race. A few men actually succeeded in breaking it.

On Pluto there was activity. There was a base there for the heavily-shielded R-40's that carried the uranium ore from the mines. Behind it there were black mountains sheathed in ice, and all around it was a plain that glittered in the starlight, white with frozen air. The base itself was one vast sunken dome, for the ships and for the men who served them. But to one side was a second dome, and above it was a group of towers somewhat different from those of the base proper, squatter and more massive. This place had been used once. Since then it had lain quiet, its contents sheathed cocoon-like in protective webs.

Now men invaded it again stripping away the sheathing, checking, testing, making delicate adjustments. And underneath the dome the giant dynamos awoke, and the solid granite of the plain was shaken.

On its massive launching track, a long dark shape lay waiting.

Far out in the gulf that lies between Sol and Alpha Centauri, Kirby wished desperately that he could go someplace else, at least temporarily. "Don't they ever give up?" he said. "Don't they ever *shut up?*"

"Ain't the nature of the beast," said Pop. He added philosophically, "Have a drink."

Kirby swore. "How many bottles did you smuggle aboard? Anyway, that's not the answer." He walked up and down. "I don't mind them yakking. don't mind them screaming. I don't even mind them sending committees, as long as I can keep them off the bridge. I mind what they're doing to the men. You hear the scuttlebutt, Pop, more than I do. You know they're beginning to wonder out loud if maybe we shouldn't turn around and go back."

"Don't blame the women too much," Shari said. She was curled up in a corner of the bench that ran around part of the bridge, looking tired and bored and infinitely, infuriatingly patient. "It was never their idea to come."

Kirby knew she was right, but it only angered him more to know it. "I don't know why you want to defend them, the way they've treated you."

Shari smiled briefly. "They are beating you over my shoulder, Kirby. Partly. Partly they're envious, not of my exotic beauty, as you might suppose, but of the luxury I enjoy, being the captain's wife. Privacy. A whole glorious eight-by-ten room all to ourselves."

"Better go down and talk to them, young Kirby," Pop said. "Talk real hard, too, or they're likely to mutiny and storm the bridge, and then where'll you be?"

"He's right," Shari said. "Go. And when you talk to them, remember this. A man thinks usually in straight lines. Women think in circles. You and the others, you see the take-off and the landing, and you worry about the dark ships, but you're sure somehow in spite of everything you'll come through. The women see their discomfort now, and their sadness for all they had to leave behind, and they're afraid for themselves—but most of all, Kirby, they're afraid for their husbands and children. You see a wonderful world ahead; they see only a terrible wilderness.

36

How will they live, how will their children live, who will teach them, who will care for their health? What dreadful things may happen, and how will they be able to cope with all these troubles? That's why they want to go back, because of the safety of their families."

Kirby opened his mouth, and Shari said quickly, "We have no children, Kirby, so it's easier for us. Be patient with them."

"Well," said Kirby, without joy, "I'll try."

"Luck," said Pop cynically. "And if you're not back in half-an-hour I'll send in the rescue squad."

Kirby went out and down the passage. One watch before the ark had reached the maximum acceleration her middle-aged bones could stand, and the stern rockets had been cut. She was running now on constant velocity, in absolute silence except when one of the auxiliaries was cut in briefly by the automatic compensators to keep her on course, or by the sensor-field detector relays that guided her safely around spatial debris. After the incessant roaring he had become used to, Kirby's own footsteps sounded unnaturally loud in the stillness. He didn't like it. It gave him a feeling of cessation, of not moving, when every nerve was screaming to make speed, speed, and more speed. He wished that somebody had perfected one of those interstellar drives they had talked about, and that he had it. Might as well wish for wings. Or luck. All he had was an elderly ship and conventional rockets, and it was going to be a long trip. Unless it was a very short one.

He went down a winding ladder to the cargo deck. It ceased to be quiet. The main holds below were full of everything they had been able to latch onto and smuggle out in the fliers, added to the original cargo the *Lucy B. Davenport* had been carrying when she went into hiding. But the cargo deck had been cleared of what light stuff was in it and refilled with women and kids.

Every one of them, Kirby thought, was yelling at full lung power. Babies cried. Small children roared, in pleasure or pain, it was impossible to tell which. Family pets yelped and yowled. Half a dozen teenage girls giggled together in a corner. A boy the same age was shooting paper wads at them. Women moved here and there, doing things, doing nothing, calling their children, playing with them, smacking them. Some of them sat on the improvised bunks, sewing or caring for infants. Some of them just sat, or lay, staring stonily ahead of them. There was a faint odor of cooking.

A network of cords ran overhead, with blankets and tarpaulins fixed to them, so that the separate families might have some privacy when they wanted it. Some of the cords were hung with diapers, and rows of little pants and shirts, and men's socks and feminine undergarments. The husbands and fathers who were off duty and had no place else to go were scattered around here and there, looking dismal and not saying much. Wilson was among them. He sat humped up beside a bunk on which his wife lay in the attitude of an uncompromising corpse, staring straight up at the roof.

Kirby hesitated. He had managed to avoid this so far. He and Shari and Pop and what single men there were aboard bunked in the officer's cabins on the bridge deck, and his duty had given him an ex-

cuse to ignore the demands forwarded to him from
below to come down and be slain. The women
seemed to have fastened on him as the archfiend
and enemy, probably because he made the actual
flight possible, and because he was by circumstance
placed in supreme authority as skipper of this reluc-
tant star-ark. Now he had a cowardly desire to turn
tail and run. But it was too late. Somebody's wife,
with total disregard for shipboard etiquette, cried,
"Phil Kirby! It's about time!" And the riot began.

Kirby climbed part way up the ladder again and
roared for silence. He regretted bitterly that there
were no proper intercom systems in these freight
decks. It was undignified for a captain to shout and
wave his arms. Finally he stopped it and let the ex-
plosion of talk wear itself out.

Sally Wilson got up off her bed and stalked
through the crowd until she was directly below
Kirby. The table of voices quieted, with final cries
of, "Tell him, Sally!"

There was a tremendous assent from the women.
But it was countered by a furious "No!" from every
boy in the place, from the teen-agers down to little
ones far too young to know what they were saying
No to. Kirby grinned.

"Between your husbands and your sons, I think
you're outvoted."

Half a dozen or so active-looking girls shouted,
"Us too!"

"Good," said Kirby. "Welcome aboard." To the
women he said, "You all loved your husbands
enough to come with them. Why don't you stop being martyred about it now and help them."

"We were *forced* to come," said Sally.

"How many of you," Kirby asked, "were actually knocked unconscious and carried aboard?"

No hands went up.

"It amounts to the same thing," Sally said.

"No, it doesn't. You could have run away or screamed for help or called the police."

"We didn't have time!" Sally wailed. "Wils just walked in and . . . I could kill you, Phil Kirby. You got Wils into this."

"Wils is a grown man, Sally. He's perfectly capable of making his own decisions."

"Damn right," said Wils.

"Well," said Sally, "I don't care. If it hadn't been for you the whole thing wouldn't have been possible. If you'd said no—" She began to cry. "We were all so happy where we were. Why did you have to do this? What more could you want that you didn't have?"

Kirby said soberly, "I couldn't explain that to you. You'll have to find out for yourself." He looked at the children, standing in little mobs and watching the grownups. "Maybe it was for them, more than anything. They ought to have a chance to grow up to be men and women, not just bits of information fed to a computer."

"I've heard all that talk," said a very large young women, pushing her way past Sally. She held an enormous pink child in her arms. "My husband's full of it. Here." She thrust the child suddenly at Kirby, so that he had to grab it to keep it from falling. "Now you look at her. It's her life you're gambling with, and what you're saying is that you don't care

40

if she lives or dies. She can do without the care and safeguards and the advantages."

"You'd be surprised," said Kirby, "how many people did."

The child, alarmed by the uproar, began to howl and kick. The mother took it back. "They didn't know any better," she said. "I want my child to be safe. I don't want anything ever to happen to her. I don't want her to grow up like an animal on some God-forsaken world nobody ever heard of." Her voice rang all over the cargo deck. "I want to go home!"

Kirby waited for the resultant clamor to die down, and as he watched them he felt an emotion stirring in him for the first time and knew that it was pity. Only it was all for the wrong reasons.

"I knew it was late in the day for this," he said. "Maybe it was too late. You're all children of your time. You're old. You were born old. That's the real thing that's been taken out of people. Youth. You never had it. Perhaps you'll never find it. I'm sorry for you. But now you listen to me. There'll be no turning back. You can't go home, unless you all want to spend the rest of your lives in penal institutions, and I doubt if you do, even though they are eminently safe and protected places. For the men there's no doubt of this at all. The women might or might not get off with lighter sentences, I don't know. The children, however, would be taken away from you and given a long course of re-education in foster homes, and you would certainly never see them again. You think that over, and then I suggest that you get to work doing something constructive, like setting up schoolrooms for your kids and organizing things a little better here. Maybe you'll even find it's kind of nice to do things for yourself, instead of sitting and having them done for you."

"But," said Sally, much subdued, "but—"

The large young woman said dramatically, "For my child's sake I'd be willing."

"Oh, bull," said her husband, who was one of the three doctors aboard. "And don't be so noble with *my* life, honey."

Some of the men laughed.

Kirby said, "Don't think so much about what you've left behind. Think about what's ahead. It's a beautiful world, very much like Earth—where you were not permitted to live. You can have your pick of it. It's not inhabited. You can make new towns, a whole new country, just to suit yourselves. There'll be others along in time, too. We're not the only ones who still think freedom wasn't so bad, in spite of the risks. Your kids will grow up to be the lawmakers of a new world, the pioneers of a galactic civilization."

It sounded fine when he said it. He hoped it would work out that way.

But Sally Wilson said, "You don't know what it's like there any more than we do. Nobody's ever been there. What's the use of lying about it?"

Kirby sighed. "I thought that had been explained to you, but I'll give it to you again. Years ago the government built a special long-range base on Pluto and sent out from it a robot starship. It was strictly a reconnaissance flight. They wanted to know what was out there, and whether it held any threat to System security. The information the R-ship brought back was never made public, naturally. But those things have a way of getting out. I've seen clips from the films taken by automatic cameras, and photostats of data concerning atmosphere, gravity, temperatures, the works. Alpha Centauri has an A-1 habitable planet. Does that satisfy you?"

"I'll believe it," Sally muttered sulkily, "when I see it. And how long will we be shut up in this smelly old trap?"

"Well," said Kirby uncomfortably, "quite a while."

"That's no answer. Weeks? Months? Years?"

"Years. About five of them. Our velocity is something under the speed of light."

Too much under. The thoughts ran swiftly through Kirby's mind: the question is, do we have enough head start? Once we land we'll be safe. Scatter and hide. A planet's a big place. But if we miscalculated, if they overhaul us—

"Five years?" Sally was saying. "Five *years?*"

"We've got supplies, if we're careful with them. We have doctors, nurses, and a stock of drugs. We—"

But suppose, he thought, we did miscalculate, and suppose our emergency plan doesn't work? Suppose something goes wrong with the ship, with the oxygen supply, or the water, or suppose we're hulled by a hunk of drift too big to patch up after. And then, oh God, what will we have done? The women had a choice, at least. But the kids—

He looked at the fat child straddling the large young woman's ample hip. It stared back at him, pop-eyed, smearing tears over its face with a grubby palm. Its nose was running. It snuffled, and suddenly Kirby was overcome with awe and horror and a sense of guilt.

43

Somebody shrieked in anguish. "Five years? You mean that for five long solid years I've got to stay in this room with—"

Voices.

"Joe Zimmerman, what did you mean, telling me it wouldn't take long? Joe, you come back here and answer me!"

"But I didn't bring nearly enough clothes . . ."

". . . no decent kitchen, and those awful beds . . ."

". . . no privacy, you can hear every word that's said . . ."

". . . have a baby *here?*"

". . . but I'll be an *old woman* before I ever *see* this world!"

Bedlam.

Kirby fled up the ladder, back to the safety and quiet of the bridge. He took the bottle away from Pop Barstow and had himself a long drink. Then he grinned.

"Well," he said, "they've quit wailing, at least. Now they're fighting like wildcats. That's a good sign, isn't it?"

Pop Barstow said, "Like the feller said, young Kirby, you have only just begun to fight!"

V

In the gulf that runs from Sol to Alpha Centauri there were now two ships.

One was far ahead. But the second ship was pos

sessed of an infinite patience and a greater speed. With every space-league the gap between them grew a little smaller.

On the second ship there was a silence, within and without. Nothing human lived in it. There was no need of anything human. The ship was sufficient unto itself. From its dark hull the sensor field spread wide, infinitely sensitive, tirelessly inquisitive. It touched an object, plunging nearer on an oblique course. Through its external contact-points the sensor-field transmitted a series of impulses to the "bridge"—the walled heart, the protected mind, the cold precise soul of the ship. There were brains there, large and small, cybernetic brains of transistors and coils and wires, whose thought was a swift shuttling of electrons. They thought, now. With inhuman swiftness they evaluated the information, set up curves and plotted vectors on the computers, and reached their conclusion. Object, meteor. Course, collision.

The cold, limited, unfrightened minds acted.

A message was flashed to relays, which sprang instantly alive. Throttles opened. The port lateral generators produced blasts of energy. The ship, moving at a velocity just under the speed of light, changed course—not a fraction too much, not a fraction too little.

The meteor went safely past. The relays clicked again. The compensators hummed. There was another little burst of energy. On a master panel red needles on several dials crawled back until they were once more contact-aligned exactly with the black ones that monitored the course. The necessity for the thought passed, and the cybernetic brains ceased to think. And again, the all-pervading silence fell.

No passengers, no crew. But the ship carried a cargo. Ranked in the nether darkness, their atomic warheads pointing down the launching tubes, the missiles slept and waited, until their own relay systems should call them to go forth and fulfill themselves.

In the RSS-1, peace and no time.

In the *Lucy B. Davenport,* far too much time and no peace at all.

Lying in his bunk, Kirby tried to sleep and failed. From across the tiny cabin Shari's even breathing mocked him. She seemed able to detach herself from her surroundings and exist undisturbed inside a kind of cocoon of patience that he envied but could not emulate. In the darkness Kirby lit a cigarette and swore inaudibly, and felt old beyond Methuselah.

Time.

Chronometer. Calendars. Clocks. Days with no sunrise, nights with no moon. Arbitrary segments cut from a universal blackness, formlessness, nothingness. Segments cut and shaped into little symbols and named with names that had no longer any meaning. What is Monday, in the spaces between the stars?

Time.

I should have done this when I was young, thought Kirby. I was sure of myself then. Now I don't know. I don't know at all. And I've got 'em here, the whole howling lot of 'em. Say the other men are as much to blame as I am, we were all in it together, made the plans and did the work and took the chances all the same. Okay. But it all hung on a pilot, and that's me. Pop Barstow is too old. Joe Davenport—and *he* was the start of it all, this was his ship and he hid her out of love and kept her safe and started the whole plan—he's been dust on the Martian wind for years now. There aren't any young pilots any more, except the ones I've trained myself right here aboard. That's why the voyage had to be made pretty soon, or never, because there aren't too many pilots left. So it was up to me. I did it. If it wasn't for me they'd all be sitting safe at home right now.

Time.

Computers. You know your own velocity. You know the top potential of the R-ship. You know the distance. You figure as near as you can how long it takes to get that particular R-ship out of mothballs and in shape to go. You pare down even that interval, so as to be sure you're not giving yourself an edge you don't have. You feed all this stuff into the computer and you get an answer, and you still don't know. You can't be sure. It's too close. You just have to sit and wait and sweat and pray, and it's one hell of a feeling.

The cigarette was burned down to his fingers. He ground it out very carefully and reached for another, and then stopped. Presently there would not be any more cigarettes, and there was no use pushing it. Shari's peaceful breathing began to rasp on his nerves. He wanted to wake her up and make her sit and twitch with him, but he fought down that desire too. Instead he got up and pulled on his pants and crept out without making any sound.

Outside in the corridor he stood for a moment trembling, thinking how it would be if anything happened to her. One in a million, she was. If they made it, if things worked out, they could still have kids. It wasn't too late.

Or was it? How close? his mind asked. How close is that black shadow behind you in the void, the shadow you haven't seen or heard but that you know is there, the swift shadow following?

He went forward to the bridge. Pop Barstow slumbered on the bench, and in the co-pilot's seat young Marapese, still too new to his responsibilities to be bored with them, sat rigidly erect watching the bank of indicators that had said nothing for far too long a time. Radarman Shaw sat in his cubby half asleep. He needed a shave, and in repose his face bore the sulky expression of a child kept after school. Kirby walked over and kicked the bench hard where Pop Barstow was lying.

"Hell of a watch you keep," he said.

Pop grunted and sat up, blinking at Kirby. "Too conscientious," he said. "That's the trouble with all you young fellows. Look." He pointed to Marapese and then to Shaw. "What's the good of me staying awake, too?"

"Because you're the senior officer," Kirby snarled. "Because it's customary. Because the kid's only a theoretical pilot as yet. Suppose something comes up he doesn't know how to deal with?"

"He'll wake me," Pop said reasonably. "You worry too much. That's bad. Ages a man before his time. Go back and get your sleep, Kirby. Anything happens, I'll let you know."

"All right, damn it, but stay awake!"

48

Kirby left the bridge. He started to go back to his cabin, but he had never felt less ready for sleep. He was tired, but there was a quivering restlessness on him, a sense of oppression. He did not know whether it was an honest presentiment or only the result of thinking too much about the same thing. Anyway, he could not go back into that dark little coop.

He went instead to the hatch that led to the cargo deck.

It was kept closed. You couldn't have a bunch of kids swarming around the bridge, handling things. He opened it as quietly as he could and went down the ladder. It was dark below, except for a few dim lights. It was nighttime. You knew that because a bell rang and after a while the main lighting tubes blinked off. Otherwise there was no change. There were no ports in the cargo deck, but if there had been it would have made no difference. What was outside had not altered since the day when, as a sort of afterthought, He made the stars also.

Kirby stood on the ladder and listened.

A child was crying, somewhere at the far end of the deck. People snored and turned and whimpered in their sleep. It was warm. The air was pure enough, but it had a stale flat taste from being breathed too many times and run through chemicals and across the hydroponic tanks. It smelled in here, of people and washing and cooking and babies. Especially babies. Especially babies.

The child stopped crying. The muffled stirrings and sighings blended into a dim monotone. Kirby took hold of the iron rail. For some reason he had begun to shake. The air was heavy. The curtained cubicles wherein the families slept looked queer and shadowed in the dimness. The people were all hidden. There was not a human face. It was as though he stood alone, and underneath his feet the ship seemed weighted with a dreadful burden.

Suddenly he turned and sprang up the ladder.

Shari was in the corridor. He thought she had been waiting for him beside the hatch. He looked at her and then past her, his eyes bright and hard, with an unnatural wideness.

"I'm going to turn back," he said.

"No."

"Damn it," he said roughly, "don't tell me no. I'm going back. I can't lead them all to the slaughter. Thought I could. I can't. We'll never make it. We haven't a chance in hell of making it. At least in prison they'd live. And the kids—they'd be all right."

"Kirby, listen." She put her hands gently on his shoulders. "Don't be afraid now when it's too late. You had a great thought."

"Who am I to have great thoughts? I'm going back."

"Kirby—"

"Shut up! Don't argue with me." He was shaking all over, hard, and he couldn't stop. He had never felt like this before. It scared him. The iron walls of the corridor bent and wavered, and the deck moved under his feet. "I've got to get them back. I—"

"Kirby, they want you on the bridge."

Her voice. Her quiet voice. Death, destruction, the hammer stroke, the end. He turned his head. There was no corridor now, no iron wall, the outer darkness had crept in and covered everything except her face. And it was close, and pale, and strange, and the eyes in it were shining.

50

He said, in a voice that was not his own, but very softly, "They haven't called me."

"They will."

The paleness and the blur that were Shari moved toward him and touched him with living lips, and his own flesh was cold, cold.

Someone was coming down the corridor, coming fast.

Kirby straightened up. The steps rang loudly against the metal, a man's steps, running.

Kirby waited.

It was Marapese. He was a young man and ashamed of fear, and he was trying not to show it, but when he spoke the words stumbled and stammered in his throat.

"Sir, Shaw says—" Pause. Tighten the lips and swallow and try again. "On the radar, sir—"

"All right." Kirby's voice was easy. It was confident, soothing, even jovial. He didn't know where it came from. He nodded to the hatch. "We don't have to tell them just yet. Shari, see about some coffee for us, will you? We'll be on the bridge." He put his hand on Marapese's shoulder. The hand was steady as a rock. It seemed to be not his own hand, but it was steady and it would do. The shoulder underneath it quivered. Kirby said, "Come on."

He walked forward toward the bridge. He felt hollow inside, there was nothing to him but a shell, but no one could see that deep but Shari, so no one would know. Marapese glanced sidelong at him, a glance of worship. His own backbone stiffened and grew straight.

Behind them, Shari smiled.

Kirby and the boy came into the bridge. Shaw

was hunched over the scope. Pop Barstow stood with one hand on the pilot's chair, his eyes riveted on Shaw, like one uncertain whether to go forward or back, and he was an old man. Kirby had never realized before how truly old he was.

Shaw said, "It's a long way off, but it's . . ." he hesitated. ". . . *it*."

"Yes," said Kirby. He glanced through the port of the inner bulkhead into the space where the computers were. "That's all the good *they* were to us. They didn't even come close."

Pop Barstow said, in an unnaturally dry voice, "Too many variables. We were slower than we'd hoped. The R-ship was faster."

Marapese asked, "What do we do now?"

"We stop it," Kirby said, as though it were the simplest thing in the world.

Marapese stared at him. "Stop it?" he repeated. "Stop an R-ship?"

Pop Barstow laughed, a laugh of unutterable sadness. "They have a plan," he said. "I've seen it. It's a pretty plan. It looks real good, all drawn up neat on a big white sheet of paper." He sat down in the pilot's seat and looked at Kirby. "You know what? We were crazy, and I was crazier than the rest of you. I was old enough to know better." He shook his head. "I'd have liked to live a while longer. Young folks think it doesn't matter to folks like me, but even when you're old you like living."

Kirby did not speak. He seemed to be thinking very hard. Shaw squirmed and sweated over the radarscope. Marapese, very pale now, looked at them.

Shari came in with the coffee.

Kirby looked up suddenly, and Shari set the tray

down with such violence that the metal cups rattled. "No," she said. "I couldn't do that, Kirby, it isn't the same."

Kirby said slowly, "A cybernetic brain isn't so different from a human one. The principle is the same. It thinks."

The color had run out from under Shari's skin, leaving it ashen. "But you have seen, Kirby—I am only a little able; I could not do it."

A strange ruthlessness had risen in Kirby. "It might give us the edge we have to have. Pop's right, the plan we've got is so much for the birds, unless we add something to it."

Marapese stared at Shari's stricken face, not understanding. But Pop Barstow understood, and was shaken.

"It don't seem right or human," he muttered, "but it might work. It might."

Kirby said to Shaw, "Keep tracking it. We need an absolutely accurate check on course and velocity. I'm going down to get Wilson and Krejewski." And Oh God, he thought, I've got to tell them all, and when they hear it—

He got the surprise of his life, when he went below and told them. He spoke as casually as he could to Wilson, and to Krewjewski who had spent his adult life building and repairing R-ships, and to Weiss, who had been a junior assistant in the Cybernetic Division. He spoke, and braced himself for the outcry.

There wasn't any. Sally Wilson began to cry, and Mrs. Krejewski took her by the shoulder in what was half a shake and half a comradely gesture of comfort. "They have to go," she said. "Don't make it

any harder for them." Then she turned to Kirby.
"Just don't come back without my George, that's all."
Kirby looked into her eyes and thought that if anything did happen to George it had better happen to
him, too. It would be easier.

He herded his three lagging heroes ahead of him
to the ladder, and all around him the women were
quiet, quieter than he had ever known them. One
small child said shrilly, "What's the matter, Mom-
my?" And her mother said, "Nothing, dear, go back
to your play." As he climbed the ladder he could
hear the normal child noises resuming. But underneath them there was still a quiet that made the
roots of his hair prickle.

He was still shaking his head when he got back
to the bridge. "I thought they'd all have hysterics,"
he said. "They didn't. Not one of 'em."

Pop Barstow grinned a little. "I told you you don't
understand women, young Kirby. They'll make your
life miserable over some little bitty thing that
doesn't matter, but when something really big comes
along they've got more guts than we have." He nodded. "Look at Shari."

Kirby looked. Her face was pale, but no longer
stricken. "Still afraid?" he asked her.

"Yes. But I see that I have to try. And I would
rather go with you than stay behind." She added,
very earnestly, "Don't trust in me too much. I don't
know that it can be done at all, and if it can, I don't
know whether I will read it right."

"You'll be okay," Kirby said, with a fine simula-
tion of casual confidence. "Pop, take them along, get
them ready, and give everything a final double-

54

check. Everything. Take your time; don't hurry it. I've got to work out the timing and the course."

He turned to Shaw, and ultimately to the computers. Velocity of *Lucy B. Davenport*, so much. Velocity of R-ship, so much. Differential. Rate of approach. Course of *Lucy B. Davenport*. Course of R-ship, which cannot possibly fire its missiles ahead of it because it is already travelling at absolute top under the speed of light and has therefore to parallel and head the slower ship, releasing its missiles on a reverse arc. Relative position of two ships now, plus mean distance on plane of flight, plus potential velocity of life-skiff, plus estimated relative position of—

You plot the parallelograms on nothing, you look at the figures and they are only figures, not realities. The realities are Nemesis, and fear, and human beings trapped in an iron trap, and folly, and a dream.

You plot the parallelogram, and it is only the beginning.

The R-ship is intelligent. It is wary. It will not permit a skiff, or a man, or a chunk of cosmic drift to get closer to it. The sensor field provides a barrier, a defense impossible to penetrate. So you think again and figure again. You extend the short line in the parallelogram that is the projected course of the life-skiff, and you add to it so many degrees of arc after it heads the still unfinished long line that is the course of the approaching R-ship. And then you bend that long line inward and then outward again in a swift apex, and you make a circle at that apex, a circle on nothing which will enclose the lives of Wilson and Weiss and Krejewski, of Shari and yourself. And if you have not forgotten how, you pray.

55

When there is no more value either in figuring or prayer, you rise and go.

The corridor seemed curiously foreshortened. There seemed no distance at all between the bridegroom and the place where the port life-skiff was housed, an iron embryo in an iron womb. The others were already inside. Pop helped Kirby on with his space suit.

"Everything's right," Pop said. "I checked real careful. All the tools and stuff."

Kirby looked down at the bulky suit. "I hoped we wouldn't have to use these things. Oh, well. Put Fenner on the radio and see he keeps it wide open. I want contact all the way."

He climbed into the skiff and took the controls. The lock sealed. A roar, a grinding, a whistle and a leaping shock, and they were free. The booster jets howled, briefly doubling the normal rocket-thrust to break the gravitational pull of the mother ship.

Behind Kirby, Shari sat very stiff and silent.

Kirby paid no attention to the others. He was too scared himself. He set his course, repeating the coordinates over aloud. He had Wilson check them too, just to be on the safe side.

"Kirby." Wilson's voice was a little raw. "Kirby, why did they have to drive us to this? They're human, like us."

"Yes. But they're dedicated to a status quo. If we licked the R-ships and made it to a new world, too many people would want to follow."

Wilson said, "But we'd be too far away to bother *them*. Why?"

Kirby shook his head. "Nothing stays too far away forever. Forget about it. Shut up."

The skiff rushed on, making the first leg of its appointed course. The rockets drummed. Kirby glared at the indicators. The others sat, in quiet agony, in stolid dread.

Presently Kirby said, "Time. Secure your helmets and check oxygen flow. Everybody's audio working? Okay." He switched on the small but very powerful communication unit built into the suit and spoke briefly to Fenner aboard the *Lucy B. Davenport*. "Clear both ways. One of us will be in contact with you from now on. We're going out now."

Wilson made one sound that might have been a sob.

Kirby cut in the starboard laterals, throttled down to one-quarter maximum thrust. Moving fast now, he saw that the space-line was secure, the long line that strung four men and one woman together like bundles on a cord. "Get your hand rockets ready," he said, "but be damned careful how you fire them!" He added with a last-minute touch of gentleness, "Don't worry. This won't be different from an ordinary space-jump for salvage. I've done that before."

He threw over the lever. The small lock opened and spewed them out.

VI

Kirby's heart came up and hit him under the chin and the enormous vault of stars reeled and wheeled around him, and his helmet audio was filled with the sounds of anguish from the four other shapes that rolled and sprawled and kicked in the unthinkable void.

"Get those rockets working!" Kirby bellowed.

The five hand rockets flared raggedly, and then all together. The combined push was enough. The little skiff went on away from them, alone and empty, beginning its long curve toward its final destiny.

"Just take it easy," Kirby said. "Relax. You can't possibly fall."

Not possibly. There is no place to fall to. There is nothing. You wonder why He made so much space and never used it.

Man wasn't made for this. Man was born and bred for a million years on a planet; he needs solid ground under his feet. Or else he needs the illusion of it, an iron deck, a shell to close him in so his littleness looks its normal size, so he doesn't shrink and vanish and become no more than a tiny unheard shriek in a vastness where even the stars are small.

Courage. A man is supposed to have it. But where do you go to look for courage in the deep primeval darkness where no sun shines?

"Kirby—"

"Kirby!"

"*Kirby!*"

"What do you want? You're all right. All you have to do is wait."

"But Kirby—"

"I tell you we're okay, on time, in the right place. We can't miss."

Can't we? Were the calculations right? Will the R-ship swerve the way we want it to, or will it do something unexpected, something clever and uncanny? It isn't right for a ship to fly itself, to think and feel as though it were alive. And it's on its own out here. Pluto base is too far away for any contact now.

All by itself. It isn't right.

Wish they had lights, like human ships. Hard to see one black blot against half the blackness in the universe, which is a lot of blackness. Kirby's eyes ached, looking into nothing, at nothing. He felt sick, and very cold. Voices spoke, and one of them was Shari's, and—

Did that star wink out?

A flicker. Another. A red streak. That's it, that's the laterals of the R-ship, its sensor-field has picked up the skiff curving round on the far side, and the so-and-so is swerving.

A thin voice cried, "It's coming right into us!"

Kirby shouted. Orders, prayers, curses. Not many. There wasn't time. A black shape loomed. It did not seem, in that weird and silent gulf, to be moving. It merely grew, without sound or rush or roar. It was small. It grew and was large. It was enormous. It was close beside them.

It has sensed us, Kirby thought, but it's overrun its ability. It can't swerve two ways at once, and in avoiding the skiff it's come right into us. So far so good, but fast now, make it fast! There won't be any other chances, and this is no place to be left behind.

Hand-rockets. Tiny sparks in the overwhelming All. Magnetic grapples, clanging hard on the cold metal, only there is no clang, it's as quiet as a deaf man's dream, and there are stars over and under and all around, except where the solid blackness is beneath your feet.

It's swerving again, to get away from these five little intruders into its sensor-field. There is still no sense of motion, but you can feel the change of direction. The grapple lines come taut. Old Man Inertia again, but this time he isn't big enough and a burst from the hand-rockets takes care of him. The lines slack again, the magnetic plates on your iron boots bite strongly. You have outwitted an R-ship. It is a triumph few men have achieved.

Few men? No men, until now.

You are weak. The blood, the bone, the guts have run out of you. You merely cling, and stare at the emptiness where you might so easily have been left, and tell Fenner inanely over the radio, "We made it."

The hull shuddered slightly. Kirby thought, "It's trying to *shake* us off, like a dog!" A wave of superstitious horror lifted the hair on his head and then he saw the space-suit that had Weiss' name on it pointing astern, where a slim torpedo shape had begun its journey with a dignified, terrible deliberation.

"It's taking care of the skiff," Weiss said.

"Yeah," said Kirby. First things first. The cold neat brains. First the skiff, and then—us. "Okay, Krejewski, Wilson—it's your show. Take over."

Shari had been silent, very silent since they had begun their clinging to the dark hull. Now she spoke, saying Kirby's name hesitantly.

"Are you getting anything?"

"I don't know. Something. Cold and strange. It's not like human thought at all. Very cold, and clear like one single note, if I could only read it. I think it knows we're here."

"The sensor-field would have told it that," said Weiss. "It sends all the data on everything it touches to the cybernetic control center in the bridge, where the information is correlated and—"

"I think," said Shari, "It hates us."

Again the chill of superstition crept and crawled in Kirby's nerves. He said angrily, "Don't go imagining things. It's only a machine. It can't feel."

"I suppose it can, in a way," Weiss said slowly. "As a safeguard against sabotage, against just what we're doing now. They're built that way, to regard humans as a menace. All their power has to be cut off before we can get in the ships on the ground, to sevice them."

Kirby growled, "Three experts and a telepath ought to be able to out-guess one lousy mechanical brain." It sounded good. He tried hard to believe it.

Wilson and Krejewski had been unhooking the cutting-torches from their belts. Wilson said nervously, "Might as well cut in here as anywhere. We'd never crack the doors. But remember these things have got automatic repair devices, so get in fast when we hole through. Now stand clear."

Out in the void that they had left behind, bright period to his words, a flare lit up the eternal night, burned savagely, and was gone.

"There goes the skiff!"

Kilson said again, "Keep clear."

The others moved back to the limit of their slack on the long line. The small hypnotic flicker of the torch-flames ate away at the metal.

Kirby questioned Shari. She only answered, in a queer remote voice, "It's still thinking."

Krejewski suddenly yelled as the metal they were cutting bulged up under them. The lines snapped taut as the others pulled them back, and there was all at once a big ragged hole in the ship's flank. And the ship stirred inwardly, as though it could feel the wound, as though the fine-drawn nerves of platinum that threaded all its bulk were carrying a message of pain.

Krejewski grunted. "Air blew out. The interior compartments will seal off automatically. Air pressure and temperature have to be kept constant. These sensitive gadgets don't do well in a vacuum at absolute zero."

"Quit gabbling and get in," Wilson said.

Kirby thrust himself into the hole. The knife-edge beam of his belt lamp slashed into the blackness, picking out the enormous ribs of the ship, touching a network of steel struts and braces.

Shari said abruptly. "Something is coming. The . . . the brain of the ship has sent it. It doesn't think for itself, I don't know what it is."

"An automatic welder, to patch this hole," said Wilson. "Hurry!"

Kirby glimpsed movement in the interior darkness. He pulled with all his strength on the rope that linked him to Weiss. A flash of Weiss' belt lamp lit the thing that was coming, a thing moving ponderously on gliding bands of magnetized metal, a huge distorted spider crawling toward the hole.

Weiss came through, with Shari's feet almost on his shoulders. They were pushing each other from outside now, in a panic. Shari was in, and Wilson came through with three pairs of hands hauling hard, and Wilson pulled frantically on Krejewski's boots.

"The thing's stopped," shrilled Weiss. "Right at the edge of the hole, right beside us."

It's measuring, Kirby thought. Give it a second or two to determine the size of the hole, and—damn these robots! Damn every one that was ever made, right back to thermostats and laundromats and self-turning-off ovens. Men ought never to have surrendered to machines? What the hell's keeping Krejewski? I never knew he was thirty feet high.

He wasn't, of course. He was only man-high, and he came in swiftly through the hole, but it was a near thing, even so. The calculating circuits in the welder had finished their computation. From out of its unlovely body it produced a steel plate of the proper size and clapped it over the hole, clearing Krejewski's helmet by less than a foot. He was barely out of range of the backlash when the welding flames went into action.

There was a catwalk. The humans worked their way to it and clung there, watching while the inexorable machine welded them securely inside the R-ship. No one mentioned that. Their thoughts were too unpleasant for utterance.

Finished with its duty, the welder moved away, returning to whatever place it occupied in the dark silence of the hull when it was not needed. Krejewski muttered, "Wait until the air is replaced in this section. That will unseal the bulkhead doors."

They waited. Kirby's heart pounded fast and hard. He was sweating inside his suit. Presently the hard-edged lamp beams softened and diffused. There was air again. He opened his helmet. The air was warm, stale, unused, unbreathed, tainted with inhuman smells of metal and oil and plastics and hot glass.

Shari's face emerged from the obscurity. "It knows

63

we're here inside it," she whispered. "Kirby, it *does* hate us—not as a man would hate; I've seen hate and it comes hot and bright into the mind, a red thing like fire—this is different. This is cold. Dark. It's not living, and yet it is. It knows how to destroy us, and it will."

"Can you see how?" asked Kirby.

She whimpered, and he thought she was going to weep. "If I were not so frightened, if I could keep my own mind clear." With shocking suddenness she did break into tears. "I told you I was not good enough for this. I told you not to depend on me!"

Kirby said quietly, "There was no one else."

She did not answer, and he did not know what she was thinking now. The light was better now, the air diffusing the glare of the lamps. Aft and forward ran the catwalks, and the arching braces, and the walls of gleaming metal. It was not like a proper ship. It was not made for men. The catwalks, for the use of maintenance crews, were the one small concession to them.

Kirby said, "We'd better get a move on."

Krejewski pointed. "It—what we're after—is up in the bridge."

They tried to hurry, but in that almost zero-gravity they moved like swimmers, floating, stumbling. The catwalks were floored with a yielding plastic tile, no good for magnetized boots. They seemed to be fumbling their way through a brooding metal labyrinth, and Kirby had a nightmare vision of failure, of four men and a woman trapped and dying slowly in an unmanned ship that would bear their bodies back to Sol as mute evidence of a mission accomplished. He dreaded each moment to hear the lateral rockets begin firing, to know that the ship had headed the *Lucy B. Davenport* and that it was too late.

"If we tried for the torpedoes," Wilson mumbled. "Maybe, if we could have fired them off."

"They're locked in tight," Weiss said. "And even without them, the ship could still destroy the *Lucy* by ramming."

"They can't have it under control now, not at all this distance!"

"They don't have to. The pattern of its mission was carefully programmed for it, with all the alternate methods of achieving it. The little cams and relays will do the rest."

"Shut up and bring that torch here," Kirby said. "Quick."

He was at the bridgeroom door, and it was closed and locked. A key back at Pluto base would open it, but nothing else would except brute force.

A torch bit into the metal. Wilson muttered as he played it, "Never been up this high before. Nobody but the top cyberneticists rated access to the bridge. I wonder—"

"Don't wonder."

The lock, burned through, grated and sagged. Kirby pushed the door open.

"Listen, what's that?"

Kirby had heard it too, the snick of a relay closing and a soft humming. The humming kept on.

He was looking into darkness. There were no windows in this bridgeroom. The mariner who navigated here had surer senses than sight.

He swung his lamp.

There was an odd relief about seeing what they

had all come to think of as It. One had almost imagined a great figure, a monstrous metallic face, a something. Here was only a machine. Humans had made it, humans had given it its orders. That was all. It was no more than a familiar calculating machine, the tall bank of transistor cells, the intricate complex of wiring, the shielded power leads, the vernier dials. No metal face, no staring eyes, nothing humanoid or menacing.

Nothing but a machine that humans had made, and that humans could unmake. He lifted his heavy wrench and started forward.

"Kirby, wait!"

Shari's voice had something in it he had never heard before. That, rather than the warning in her words, stopped him.

"There's danger," she said. "Wait. Don't go. I can get it—I can almost get it. It's waiting; something warned it when we came, it's—"

"Oh, hell," said Wilson.

"I'm not hysterical!" she cried. "It's hard to explain, I get it just over the limits of consciousness, but this—this thing—it's *prepared*."

Kirby felt the hairs lift on the back of his neck. "All right," he said, "we'll try it this way. Keep back."

He swung the heavy wrench and hurled it at the machine.

What happened, happened fast. The wrench, a yard from the delicate transistor banks, flew back at them with a flash of light. Weiss screamed. There was a metallic clang. Then silence.

"It hit me! I think my arm is broken," Weiss groaned.

"It threw the wrench back at us," Wilson said. His voice was hoarse. "Like . . . like . . ."

Kirby got control of his own feelings, not without an effort. "Listen. There's a force-field around it. It came on automatically when we broke in. Of course. It came on to protect it, for only intruders would break in."

"But we can't get through that," Krejewski said. "There's no way."

"So we're licked?"

Then suddenly a sweet, high-pitched note of sound rang from the ball banks of cells. Nothing else, no movement, no lights. But, almost instantly, there came the low rumble of the port laterals firing.

Kirby, at the first vibration of that rumbling thunder, dived toward the others. They were in a group close behind him. He knocked them roughly, staggering, toward the door opening. Weiss yelled as his arm hit something.

Their tangled little group wedged against the door. The ship canted sharply. It moved in a turn too sharp for any human crew to endure without warning and protection, but perfectly practicable for a ship that had no crew. It crushed them against the doorframe, Kirby desperately holding onto Shari.

The rumble of rockets stopped. The pressure relaxed. Weiss was sobbing in pain.

"It tried to *throw* us into that force-field," Wilson was saying. "Let's get out of this." He started to scramble away.

Kirby hauled him back. "Get out to where? Empty space? Not to the ark; she won't exist if we leave here now. That wasn't for us, don't you understand?

The R-ship is starting to head around. It's altering course, and that means it'll be launching its warheads at the *Lucy*, unless we stop it."

"But how? We can't get near it. We can't touch it. How?"

Kirby did not answer. He looked at the thing that lay so securely beyond their reach. He hated it. It was the symbol and the force of the power that had enchained mankind. It was everything he and the others on the ark had fought and fled from, and it had won, reaching even here into the emptiness between the stars to grasp at human aspiration and make it not. A great rage rose up in him.

"Weiss, you're the cybernetics man. Damn it, stop blubbering and listen! We can't smash it up by brute force. All right. Isn't there another way? Men build these things. They can't be smarter than men. They can't be all-powerful."

Weiss answered wearily, "They might as well be as far as we're concerned. Even if we knew the frequency and the code that controls this particular ship, it wouldn't do us any good. See that master panel?" He pointed to an assembly of dials and indicators that meant nothing to Kirby." It's different from any other I've seen, designed for a star-ship that has to be out of touch with its base, on its own. It's locked. Nothing's going to change the settings or it until the orders they represent have been carried out. Then they'll shift into the "Return to Base" position. And that's that."

"It has an order," Kirby said. "It can't disobey that order." He was fishing for an idea, a nebulou thing out of human psychology remembered from lot of long dark years. He took Weiss by the shou ders. "These cybernetic brains aren't very different from the human variety, are they? Functionally, I mean."

"No. Look out, you're hurting my arm. They're simpler, of course. Faster reaction time on a lot of things, no emotional complications, so they're more efficient, but then they're not adaptable to change, either. No, they're not basically very different."

"All right. Weiss, you and Wilson are going to figure out from watching its reactions what wavelength the thing is sensitive to. And you've got no time to do it in. Fenner? Fenner!"

The voice of the radioman on the *Lucy Davenport* spoke inside his open helmet. "Yeah, Kirby. Yeah. What's—"

"Fenner, stand by with every amp you've got. Give me a scatter band in the UH frequencies, the banned-off ones." The *Lucy's* communicator had been built before the banning, before there was no longer any need for ships to talk together across space. Near a control center it would have been drowned out by the vastly more powerful transmiter, but here in this untracked waste of nothingness it might work. It might.

"Watch it," he said to the two men hanging irresolute by the doorway. "Switch in, and give your readings direct to Fenner."

"Kirby," said Wilson, "you're crazy. But I guess doesn't matter now. I'm sorry we all did this thing, though. I should have stayed on Mars. I don't want ally and the kids to die. I don't want to die mylf."

Kirby hit him, clumsily, savagely, across the back. "hen watch it, damn you! *There!*"

A bank of transistors that had been dark glowed briefly and were dark again. Weiss began to talk, very fast, very nervous, to Fenner. Kirby got busy on the space-line. There were railings on the catwalk. He threw hitches over them, made himself and the others fast so they could not be pitched forward into that deadly room, or smashed against the struts. He took Shari in his arms and said to Krejewski, "Hang on hard. If this works, it'll be rough."

"Narrow it down," Weiss was saying. "What have you got there? No, you lost it again. Higher. That's it, I think. Oh God, my arm hurts! No, no, Fenner, try it again, slower, hold it—hold it! It's receiving now but it isn't reacting; what good is the frequency without the code word? It could be anything." A gray flatness had come into his voice, and Kirby knew that it was the sound of despair. "Run through the alphabet," Weiss said. "Fast. Maybe—"

Again that one sweet note rang out, and then there was the following thunder of the laterals. Again the terrible hand of inertia struck them, crushed them, left them dazed and gasping.

"Hurry it up," said Kirby. "Hurry."

Wilson wept and cursed him. Weiss, half conscious in the doorway, was muttering his ABC's.

"M, N, O—no reaction yet, go on—P, Q, R, S—S Hold it, Fenner! There was a flicker on S. It's waiting for the rest of the word."

"The rest of the word," said Wilson. "There's million of 'em beginning with S."

"Try STAR," said Kirby.

It didn't work.

It was Fenner who suggested STELLA.

It worked.

"Pour it on!" Kirby shouted. "Tell it to sheer off, change course."

The receiving unit glowed and a humming, soft and busy, arose in the relays of the brain.

"Hang on!"

This time it was the starboard laterals. Krejewski and Wilson yelled together in mingled anguish and delight. Weiss had fainted. Kirby, holding tight to Shari and enduring the pressure, did not exult. The burst was short. Almost at once the port laterals roared again. The locked master control and the compensators were not to be defeated so lightly. The RSS-1 was back on course again.

"Keep it coming," Kirby said to Fenner. He thought of Fenner in the communications room with Pop Barstow and Marapese and Shaw sweating it out with him. He thought of the broad-beamed *Lucy* forging sturdily ahead with her freight of human life, and how it would be when her belly split open in a burst of flame and spewed the washlines and the cooking pots, the babies and the children, the mothers and their men, all out across the black gulf to drift forever on the slow-wheeling tide of the galaxy.

Desperately, and with no real hope, he said, "Tell it to return to base. Tell it to by-pass its master circuit. I don't suppose it can, but we might at least confuse it."

Past Wilson's crouching shape he could see the glow and flicker of the banked transistors. Celebration, naked and visible. Fenner's voice spoke in his ears, remote and twanging like a taut wire. "Shaw says it's getting awful close to us. What's it doing here?"

The starboard laterals swung the ship over in a vicious arc. Kirby braced himself. "It's beating us to death," he gasped, "but that's all right, that's what I want—" One breath, one burst of speech, before the compensators took over. "Pour it on!"

Krejewski whispered, "We can't take much more of this."

Fenner's voice muttered in Kirby's ear, "Return to base. Return to base." He was talking to himself, to his transmitter key, to God, while the *Lucy's* generators labored to make strong that silent voice that spoke from her across the void to the R-ship. *Return to base.*

Shari, who sagged in Kirby's arms, like a limp rag doll, lifted her head and said, "It's confused. It—if it were human it would scream; it suffers, it has pain." She quivered and clung to him. "Hold me, I'm afraid!"

Thunder. Chaos. Pressure. Vertigo, a gasping and a straining and a cry, five small soft humans crushed and trapped between titanic forces. The laterals boomed and kicked, fighting each other, hurling the ship into a mad pinwheel flight that spiralled wildly nowhere. Kirby, blinded, deafened, barely conscious, cried triumphantly, "Pour it on!" The darkness was full of sound, the pain-cries of metal strained to the limit of its strength.

In the bridgeroom, in the brain, something blew.

Convulsion, the throes of death. It can't be dying Kirby thought, it never lived, it's only an iron hulk, cold thing, soulless, so why does it kick and lash itself about like a living thing in agony?

Shari wailed, a weird high keening, and over that and beyond it Kirby heard the strands of the brai

72

parting, the snap and the tearing and the brittle, delicate crack of a million tiny cells falling in minute shards.

And suddenly it was very still.

Shari whispered, "It's dead." She was weeping. "It couldn't understand. Kirby, it knew, and at the end it was afraid. It was afraid of its own madness."

Kirby shook his head. He did not want to admit that what she said was true. "It wasn't human," he said, and then he thought, but wasn't that a human trick we played on it? Give it orders it can't possibly obey, impulses it can't possibly satisfy, and what happens? What happens to the infinitely more complex, more flexible and reasoning brain of a man, when it is tortured with conflicting problems it cannot solve? It splits wide open. The doctors have a name for it, but names don't matter. We have just lived through the actuality.

And it was dead, and the ship was only a drifting wreck.

Kirby got up. He set Shari aside and freed himself from the rope, and stumbled forward over the squirming, groaning bodies of men who were, miraculously, still alive to squirm and groan. He went into the bridgeroom.

It was silent. It had always been silent, but now there was no Presence in it. Kirby got his hands on something and threw it. It crashed with a bursting tinkle into the master panel, where the dials remained unaltered, inexorable in authority. The force-field was gone. Kirby picked up the wrench that had broken Weiss' arm. For a moment he ceased to be Kirby, or any other man. He was rebellion. He was all the people in the ark. He was

73

the people who would follow them in other ships. He was the might and the power of his kind, the unpatient ones who will not wear chains forever, no matter how they are ornamented and disguised. He walked forward to the master control and smashed it. It was a purely symbolic gesture, quite useless but somehow immensely satisfying. The inexorable needles broke and skewed, the dial faces fell awry, and Kirby smiled. Then he let the wrench drop. He turned and left the bridgeroom, slowly, because he was tired and his battered body hurt.

"Come on," he said, "come on, we still have to cut our way out of this." Into the radio, to Fenner, hysterical on the other end, he said, "Tell Pop to get over here and pick us up."

He roused up his army of four and stumbled away the catwalk in the silence and the dark.

VII

After the death of the R-ship—and somehow Kirby could never think of it any other way—the road to the stars was clear. The *Lucy B. Davenport* trundled and slovened on toward the distant beacon of Alpha Centauri that seemed never to grow nearer. Life settled to a kind of weird normality, with fewer frictions and complaints than Kirby would have believed possible. Shari said it was because everyone had expected to die when the R-ship caught up with them, and now they were just thankful to be alive. Pop Barstow said it was because people can get used to anything if they're forced to it. However it was people ate and slept and found necessary things to do in between. They played games and taught their young. Babies were born. Two men and one woman and an infant died and were buried in the deep outside. And time went slipping, sliding, gliding past in a kind of dull hypnotic fashion, unnoticed except by the chronometers. They at least knew that time was passing. To everyone else it appeared that time had stopped. So that finally when the day came Kirby could not quite bring himself to believe it.

He went down the ladder to the cargo deck. Halfway on the iron rungs he stopped and looked out over the deck, and all the people that were in it looked up at him but did not speak, and even most of the children were still.

Kirby said, "We'll land within the next two hours."

Now again as he was conscious of time. Five years. Nearly six, as Earthmen count. Five years, nearly six, in the huge cold night that lies between the suns, and the night was over and there were only two short hours left between these people and the realization of a dream.

He knew what they were thinking, sitting there in little huddles on the rows of cots, trying to keep the children safe and quiet, waiting, watching him. They were thinking, what if something happens now, at the last minute? What if all this time and distance has been for nothing, and we die?

A burst of thunder drowned out all other sounds, and the *Lucy B. Davenport* shuddered in all her iron bones. The people swayed, and Kirby could see their mouths come open, but he could not hear anything but rockets. Everything that was not bolted down moved forward along the deck or through the air. Balancing easily on the ladder, Kirby glanced with a fast professional eye at the preparations that had been made, and then he looked for Wilson and found him.

"Better secure the doors of the galley locker, Wils. If the catches tear off, you'll have the place full of pots and skillets. And there's a wash line over there," he pointed, "just set to wrap around someone's neck. Otherwise everything looks good."

Wilson nodded. He was still a young man, but he looked a hundred years old at this minute, his eyes haggard and very bright. Kirby knew what he was thinking, too. He was wishing he did not have to sweat through these next two hours. He was wishing the landing was already made and done with, and safe.

You think it's tough, Kirby thought, to have to sit down here and sweat through the landing. What about me? I have to make it.

"Get with it," he said to Wilson. "And watch out for the next blast." Wilson turned and beckoned to the other men who were part of the committee responsible for the security of the people in the cargo deck. They talked a minute and then they threaded their way between the cots to the galley where the women had done their cooking for nearly six years now and got busy with part of a coil of wire they had left from making other things fast. A woman got up and rather shamefacedly took down her washline. Washlines and diapers, Kirby thought, stewpots and soap and a smell of sour milk, and that's how you conquer the stars.

He said aloud, so they could all hear him, "The

brake blasts will come closer together now, so don't try to move around. You'll be safest if you use all your bedding to pad the cots and then strap yourselves into them. I see some of you already have—good, and the rest of you get busy and help each other. Above all, keep the kids tied down."

A note of gentleness, almost of pity, came into his voice. "And don't worry. You'll hear a lot of noise, and the ship may pitch around a good bit, but there's nothing to be afraid of."

Somewhere, anonymous in the concealment of blanket-and-pillow padding, a girl was making the sharp barking noises that precede hysteria. Nervous excitement, rather than any real fear. Some of the younger children, frightened by the unaccustomed roar and jarring, were beginning to cry in earnest. Kirby shook his head. "Try and keep them quiet," he said. "It'll soon be over." He went back up the ladder.

He closed the hatch and dogged it down. Scared, he thought. Why should they be scared? They don't know all the things that can happen on a landing, on the best spaceport with the best ship and all the best ground-control equipment there is to help you do it. They don't realize that it isn't easy to come down out of the blue and go to roost in some bramble patch like a ruddy bird. They don't realize how old the *Lucy* is, a tired old freighter already pushed far beyond her strength. She could blow her tubes. She could break up. She could misfire and just plain crash.

Kirby watched his own hands fastening the hatch. What about those hands? Could they still take a ship down, could they remember after all these years the thousand intangible things a pilot's hands must know, the time and the feel and the balance of a ship?

The all-important hands made three tries on the last dog before they could get it set.

Kirby went on to the bridge.

Pop Barstow was in the pilot's chair. An old rocket man, too old, and Kirby wished he wasn't. He wished he could leave the whole responsibility to Pop.

"Hold on," said Pop. "I ain't through yet." He punched the keys again, and they held on, Kirby and Shaw the radarman in his cubby, and Shari who was standing beside the pilot's chair looking out, looking for the new world that would be stranger to her than to the rest of them because it was not at all like Mars. The roar and the shudder came again, and the great hand of inertia slamming at them, and Kirby's ears hurt with trying to hear the individual creakings of the ship's fabric through the noise of the rockets. When things were quiet again he cursed Pop Barstow. "What're you trying to do, break her back?"

"Her back's in better shape than mine," said Pop. He slid over into the co-pilot's chair. "And anyway, young Kirby, I was flying rockets when you were kicking in your cradle. Haven't got a bottle hid away, have you?"

Kirby took the controls as though they were so many sticks of dynamite. "Hell," he said angrily, "you soaked up every drop there was three years ago."

"Pity. Best thing in the world for what you've got." He looked up at Shari. "Funk," he said. "That's what this husband of yours has got. Last-minute, end-of-the-run funk. Trouble with these young fellows now, no stamina. You'd think after everything else that a simple little landing wouldn't upset him." He shook his head slowly. "Now if I'd been able to beat out an R-ship—"

Kirby said between his teeth, "Thanks, Pop, but I'd rather you left my morale alone."

He punched the keys. When it was over Pop said quietly, "You'll have to give her more than that unless you figure on driving her right through the planet."

Kirby did not answer because he knew that what Pop said was true. He looked out the forward port. The glare-shields were in place, but even so the two suns, Alpha Centauri and the more distant companion, flooded space with a brilliance that was gloriously painful to the eye after the years of darkness. In that sea of light a planet swam, green and lovely and very like Earth, as Alpha Centauri is very like Sol. And Kirby's heart contracted with a pang of mingled pain and exultation.

Shari spoke abruptly over Kirby's head. She spoke in the old High Martian which only she and Kirby understood. "I will put it into words for you, Kirby. Your dream ends with the landing. It is sad, but there is no help for it."

"There are times," Kirby said, "when it would be better if my wife were neither telepathic nor talkative." And then he asked her what the devil she meant by that statement.

"The others," she said, "they broke the law and risked themselves and their families to make this flight because they dreamed of a world where

79

thought and action should be free, and not forever bound by government decree. You, beloved, you thought highly of these things too, but it was only a thought. Your dream was to go to space again, to hold a rocket ship between your hands once more before you died. So now you have done it. Now your dream ends, and theirs begins."

She leaned over and kissed him quickly, gently, and turned away. "Let it be enough that you are the first spaceman to span the stars. A big thing, Kirby. A very big thing, but not good at all without a landing. Make it."

She went out of the bridge before Kirby could think of any adequate words.

He sat for a moment watching the beautiful green planet sweep toward him, furious because of the implications in what she had said and at the same time wondering if she could just possibly be right. Then all he could think of was the men and women and kids down there under hatches with their lives depending on him, and how scared he had been at the take-off for the same reason. Then he really got mad. He said aloud, "I'll show her." He hit the brake-jets again, and again, and a third time in close succession, hard, and he said to the *Lucy B. Davenport*, "All right, you old cow, if you're going to break up do it now!"

And he repeated, "I will show her."

In the co-pilot's chair, Pop Barstow grinned a fleeting, nervous grin. He braced his feet as though he meant to push them through the deck plate, and waited.

Kirby took her down.

Part of the time he knew what he was doing, and

part of the time his hands and his eyes teamed up and worked by themselves, getting messages from the instrument bank and from the deep inner pulse of the ship and combining them into a single truth expressed in terms of velocity and thrust.

He knew where to land. The spot had been chosen from what they had seen of the data brought back by the RSS-1. To a robot ship, bitterly enough, belonged the honor of the first interstellar flight, and the only consolation Kirby had for that was that the R-ship had paid with its life for that piece of insolence. The information brought back from the reconnaissance flight had been kept secret, of course, but secrets have a way of getting out when enough people are determined to know them, and on one clip of smuggled microfilm a place had been shown that looked well-nigh perfect for a colony. The knowledge that there was a habitable world in the system of Alpha Centauri had sparked this whole odyssey of the *Lucy B. Davenport*. Without that certainty she would have remained in her hidden cave in the Martian sea bottom until her own red dust was indistinguishable from the red sand.

Kirby checked his coordinates and rolled on over the curve of the world, from the night side through the dawn belt and into the light of day, dropping lower with that splendid tearing thunder that only a rocket has. The seas were blue beneath him, and the forests green, and it was almost like the landings he had made on Earth long ago, except that the continents were differently shaped.

He picked up the landmark in the south temperate zone, a mountain range with three great peaks in line. He crossed them, with the white snow throwing back the sunlight at him like a giant's heliograph. There were miles of forest, and then a plain with a river running through it, a wide slow river as huge and grand as the Mississippi. There were game herds on the plain. They ran from the sound of the rockets, raising a mighty cloud of dust. Awe and disbelief came over Kirby. He set the ship down very carefully as though it were a thing of glass, so carefully that the nerve ends all over his body hurt with the agony of achieving that precision, and she was at rest in a bend of the river.

The rockets were stilled, and there was a kind of terrible silence. Kirby listened to it, and knew that at least part of what Shari had said was true.

The smoke and the hot dust settled or blew away. He could see out the port again. He looked, sitting in the pilot's chair with his hands still on the controls, not moving, feeling like someone who has just died. His nerves did not hurt any more. His head did not ache. Nothing felt at all. Five years, he thought. Nearly six, in space, with an R-ship to hunt us down. And there were all the years before that, working on the *Lucy* in secret, lying, stealing, risking our necks every day and every night, and all of it aimed straight at this final moment, this *now*, that none of us ever really believed we'd reach. And we have reached it. We are here, and safe.

He thought, I did it. Not taking anything away from the others, but ultimately it was me, Kirby, that told them how to fit the ship, and took her off, and flew her, and set her down. I did it. And I did it well.

Feeling came back to Kirby. A weakness in the

knees, a wild pounding of the heart and a general unnamed and nameless warmth that filled him like fire in the night. He looked out at the new world. It was a good, big world, with horizons all around it, wide open to Andromeda and beyond. He was content.

"Go let 'em out, Pop," he said, "before they burst out through the seams."

Pop didn't answer. Kirby turned his head. The old man was sitting there with a dazed look and two undeniable tears in his eyes. His lips were moving, and presently Kirby understood that he was saying, over and over again, "I never thought we'd make it. So help me God, I never thought we'd make it."

Kirby got up, staggering a little because the tension had all run out of him and left his muscles loose. He put his hand on Pop's shoulder. "You old so-and-so," he said. "Didn't you trust me?"

Pop shook his head. "You're a good rocket man. So was I, once. But that wasn't enough. We needed miracles. One at the take-off, to beat the R-3's. One to take care of the RSS-1, and that was a big miracle, Kirby, a real king-size spectacular. And then maybe the biggest miracle of all, just to hold together and get here and come down all in one piece. Three miracles. That's too many."

"Well, we had 'em. And now we don't need any more."

A long slow shudder slid through the bones and wiry muscles of the shoulder under Kirby's hand. "Unless they send more R-ships after us. More robot ships to hunt us down."

Kirby said furiously, "Oh, for God's sake." He took his hand away, before he used it to break Pop Bar-

83

stow's neck. "Look, we just made a landing; we're alive, let us enjoy it a little before you start crying up more woe!"

Pop said wearily, "When you get to be my age, you learn never to trust things when they're going too good."

"That's a fine line of reasoning," Kirby snarled. "I suppose it would be better if we were all dead." He stamped out of the bridge, all the exultation gone from him. Shari was waiting for him in the corridor. He jerked his head toward Pop inside, and said, "Why does he want to be like that?"

Her voice shook a little when she answered, and he saw that her habitual Martian calm was stretched very thin. "None of us is quite sane at this moment. We take it out in different ways. Listen!"

He listened. Below deck and now, it seemed, from outside, there sounded a howling and whooping and clamoring that was the damndest noise Kirby had ever heard, like people laughing and crying and praying and having hysterics all in one breath. He shook his head, smiling uncertainly. Without knowing it he had taken hold of Shari's arms, and his fingers were sunk deep in the flesh.

"I did it," he said.

"Yes."

"And it wasn't all because I wanted to go to space again, Shari. I want others to go to space, too. I want to save—" The words became confused with the violence of what he felt. Courage and pride, he was trying to say, the man-virtues that are almost gone. These I wanted to save. The uproar from below rose and rocked him. "Who let them out? I was just going to open the hatch."

"The young Shaw. He ran there as soon as the keel touched."

"Without waiting for orders. The young whelp! Oh well, that's the end of orders, anyway. They're on their own now."

He shifted his grip until she was pulled in tight against his chest, so tight that it was hard for both of them to breathe. She was trembling. He kissed the top of her head, thinking vaguely how beautiful she was and how much he loved her, thinking, Damn Pop Barstow and his croaking! And Shari answered him without waiting for his question, "Yes, I was afraid. I have been afraid ever since we left Mars. And you are angry with the old man because you know that more R-ships may come and you don't want to think about it."

"He might have let me enjoy the landing."

"The old live always with their fears." She tried to pull away, laughing in a choked-up, unfamiliar way. "Kirby, you will suffocate me! Let us go outside and stand on the ground and breathe the air. Let us get out of this hideous, this awful hateful ship!"

She said that last with such passion that he was astonished. She ran away from him down to the corridor, to the ladder that led to the hatch. He blinked and went after her. They were practically alone in the ship now. Everybody had stampeded for the open, scattering out beyond the charred and smoking circle the landing jets had made, to where the prairie grass grew thick and green.

They were doing things that Kirby had never seen adult men and women do before unless they were wild drunk. The children screamed and ran and rolled in the grass and the wild-flowers, and the little ones, the ship-born babies, cried. They had never seen a world and a sky, and they were frightened. For them, it was like a second birth.

Shari was still ahead of him. She mingled with the group and he lost her in it because suddenly people were hanging on him and crying and pounding him on the back, and even the most vocal of the women who had made the voyage under protest for this one brief moment loved Kirby next to life itself.

Here and there, on the edges of the crowd and in it, people began to go down on their knees.

Nobody said anything, nobody led the movement, but it spread and the crowd got quieter, and finally it was all quiet and everybody was kneeling, or standing with a bowed head. And Kirby saw Shari, far out on one side where the prairie began to slope upward toward the foothills and the forest. She had stopped running. She was standing still.

He went to her. The air was warm, with a feel and taste of spring. His body felt heavy and pleasantly weak in the unaccustomed gravity, his feet were clumsy in the grass after the years of walking on bare cold iron. It was good. It was good to think of building a house and living here, free from acts of law that told you where to live and where to work and how many children you could have, so that the economic balance could not be upset and no change could occur—because change was always accompanied by pain for somebody, and of course pain was bad.

It was good to think of living with Shari where there was not a dead weight of social custom t stumble over everywhere they turned, because she was Martian and he was not, and that made it somehow improper that they should love each other.

He put his arms around her and told her so, not with words. She didn't need them, and thoughts were better anyway. Then he realized that she was not listening to him. She was not even looking at him, her eyes unfocused and far-away, with nothing in them but a shadow.

He asked her what the matter was. She did not answer, and after a while he shook her hard, and shouted her name. She shivered, and her head dropped forward. He thought she was going to faint, but then she said, "Kirby, please, I want to go back to the ship."

"But you were so crazy to get out of it! What's the matter with you?"

"Nothing."

"Don't give me that. Something frightened you. What was it?"

She looked from him to the kneeling people and then to the old ship that had done with flying. And she lifted her head and smiled and said, "I told you, we are all mad today. Let us not think of it again."

She began to chatter about where they would build their house, bright words with nothing behind them, pulling him back toward where the others were. He stopped that.

"What was it that frightened you, Shari?"

She began to cry, the second time in his life that he had seen her do it.

She said, "I don't know what it was. I can't tell you, Kirby, because I just don't know!"

VIII

After nearly six years of eternity, there was time
again. There were days and nights, not abstractions
marked out on a dial but actual risings and settings
of the sun, with the warm light and the cool star-
shot darkness in between. It was a fine thing to have
time back again. For quite some stretch of it the people of the *Lucy B. Davenport* went as nearly sleep-
less as possible just for the pleasure of rediscover-
ing dawn and seeing what the stars looked like with
a kindly sky between to veil them off. Alpha Centauri III lacked a moon, and they were sorry about
that. But they named it New Earth anyway, and
they loved it perhaps more than they ever had Old
Earth, simply because they had been so long without any world at all.

There was wind again, and rain, and all the smells
that come with them, with wet grass and wet ground
and then a hot sun on them to draw the steaming
sweetness out. There were clouds, and the sound of
thunder. The people of the ship stayed outside as
much as they could, sheltering under bits of canva
or nothing at all, going in only when they were
forced to. They worshipped the sun. They wallowed
and gluttoned in the light of it, soaking it in, scald
ing themselves with it until they were red as lob
sters, so greedy for it that they made no complain
about having two suns often in the sky, which mad
for double shadows and a quite un-Earthly glare.

They got muscles in their legs again, and the ship-born babies learned to walk properly, carrying their spines straight against the pull of gravity. And a queer thing happened. Kirby and Pop Barstow were rocket men, and all the others were technicians, expert worker with electricity and electronics and nucleonics and cybernetics. Not one of them had in his entire life turned a sod or planted a seed, nor had he ever felt the lack of it. Yet now, with an urge as deep and unspoken as the urge of the lemming, each one of them got hold of some sort of an implement and went out to dig with it.

There were two tractors in the *Lucy*, part of the cargo she had been carrying when her owner hid her away to evade the Government decree that all manned rockets be surrendered and broken up. They trundled these out and broke the prairie sod, scratch-ig out lopsided fields and crooked furrows in them, wearing out the books they had on Farming: How To Do It. Wearing out their hands and their backs and their tempers, driven on by nearly six years of life on iron decks, between iron walls, hungry with a terrible hunger for the soil that they had never hought of before, and never been without.

The women put in gardens and the children helped to work them, and the ship-born babies took ike small pigs joyously to the mud. And Kirby ought to have somebody look after the *Lucy's* hy-roponic tanks because it would be a long time till arvest and God alone knew what might come up.

After they planted, they began to build. And so ur, nothing had bothered them. No shape of men-ce had appeared, no voice had spoken. The auto-atic cameras of the RSS-1 had shown the planet to be uninhabited in the sense of human life, so there were no hostile natives to be feared. Even the game herds had withdrawn, not liking the noise and the activity of the unaccustomed smells. If there were large carnivores they had not come near the ship, perhaps because of the fires that burned all night around where the people were camped. But Kirby had not forgotten Shari's behavior on the day of landing. She seemed to have done so herself, but he knew her better than that, and he knew her better than to think it had all been nothing more than the nervous hysteria of the time.

There was a tributary stream that ran down from the foothills to the north, pouring into the river a half mile or so above where the ship had come down. From its bed they hauled flat stones to make foundations, and at its side, where there was a bay of slack water, they set up the sawmill they had put together during the voyage. And one evening, when he and Shari had finished laying three courses of stone, in an oblong form that was almost square at the corners, Kirby said, "We're going to start lumbering tomorrow."

"I know." She sat down on the hopeful little structure they had raised out of nothing toward being a house. She looked tired and dirty, and her knuckles were barked and bleeding. She sucked them methodically, staring at the ground.

Kirby said, "We'll be going up into the forest for the first time. There." He pointed, remembering how she had stood and the way she had been facing.

"Yes," she said. "I know."

"Do you want to tell me now what it was you saw or heard or thought, up there?"

"I can't." She hesitated, groping for words that would explain to him something he had never experienced. "It was not even thought, and yet it was, too. But—" She shook her head.

"But you had some kind of a contact. Have you had it since?"

"No."

Rather sharply, Kirby said, "You must know something about it. Is it dangerous? Is it animals or people or some life-form we never heard of?"

He shouted at him, "I don't know!"

He said down beside her. "All right, Shari. But you must know why you were afraid of it."

"Yes. I know that." And she began slowly to put words to the old nightmare they had shared between them, the thing they still dreamed about but almost never mentioned. "Do you remember the R-ship, the great brain it had, all the countless little tubes and tiny filaments and endless wiring as delicate as spider-threads?"

"I remember," Kirby said.

"When I was standing alone there, away from the others, looking toward the forest and thinking how strange and beautiful it was—it is the first one I have ever seen, except in pictures—suddenly the forest was blotted out and in my mind I saw something else. I saw the brain of the R-ship."

Kirby forgot to breathe.

"I saw it," said Shari, "from the inside."

Kirby said carefully, "From the inside? How was that?"

"First as a whole, with every tube and circuit clearly marked, and the linkages to the master controls lined out. Then, still as a whole, but with smaller things super-imposed on it, somehow staying all clear, though at the same time I could see the germanium crystals in the transistors. I could see exactly how the current flowed through circuits. I could see—structure."

She stopped, and Kirby said, "Go on."

"I could see atoms," she said, in a flat far-off voice. "I could see the particles inside the atoms. Quite clearly, Kirby. I could even see the spaces between the nucleons."

Kirby said, "My God."

He did not say anything more for a long time, and neither did she. The shadows got long, and a breeze went over the prairie, shaking the grass in wide slow ripples. Somewhere a creature that was almost, but not quite, a bird, sang an evensong composed of three sweet dropping notes.

Kirby shivered. "Total comprehension. Total visualization, total projection. And it can see inside atoms."

There was another long stillness. The far peaks turned to purple, and from the highest one a plume of snow like a white feather was blown out by a gale wind they could neither hear nor feel. The bird-creature stopped singing.

"All right," said Kirby. "Accept that. But why the R-ship's brain?"

"It—the one whose mind I touched—was trying to get in contact with the R-ship. It must have thought the *Lucy* was a robot ship, the RSS-1 come back again."

The forest grew darker and darker, creeping close onto the plain. No, thought Kirby, that's only a trick of the light, and don't let us lose our grip altogether.

Something that can see the particles inside an atom, and wants to hold converse with the cybernetic brain of a robot ship.

"Why did it want to, Shari? Was it in welcome, fear, what?"

She said miserably, "I don't know. It came so fast, a flash like a—well, like a blow on the head. I can't describe it. I saw what I have told you, and then my own fear rushed up and closed it out. I don't know what it felt, or whether it felt at all."

With sudden violence Kirby said, "Is there something else now trying to take this away from us? Do we have to fight every step of the way?" He stared at the dark forest. For a long time the RSS-1 had been *It*, the enemy, the destroyer. Now there was another one. He was sick of things called It, and this one did not even have a face or a shape to it.

But it had a brain.

He turned and took her hands, "Shari."

"No, please, Kirby."

"I'm right here, nothing can hurt you."

"Please."

"I'm going up there tomorrow. A lot of us are going. I want you to try and contact this thing again. I want to know what it is, before I risk the lives of these men."

She sat silent for a moment, quite rigid. Then she said, "Very well, Kirby." Her face became closed and secret, but her hands were gripped on his, the hands of a child waiting for the lash to fall.

Silence, and the shadows stretched and flowed until they filled the plain. The mountains put off their purple, changing to a midnight blue.

Shari's hand relaxed. She sighed and said, "It's

not there now. At least I can't hear it. There are many voices in the forest, but they say only the small animal things about fear and hunger and sleep."

"Nothing?"

"Nothing."

Kirby got up. "All right, we better get back to the ship. I'm hungry." They started to walk toward where the evening fires burned. "Don't say anything about this to the others."

"No."

"Damn it," said Kirby savagely, "I wish we had guns." Explosive weapons, like hunting and physical violence, had long been obsolete in the Solar System.

"Perhaps guns would not be any more use than the little shockers."

"Maybe not, but there was something very comforting, I remember, in just the feel of one in your hand."

He was too tired not to sleep that night, but not too tired to dream. He prowled the corridors of nightmare, angry and afraid, seeing nothing but knowing that he was seen, down to the last smallest particle of the atoms that made him. After a while he realized that he was holding a little world between his hands as a child holds a ball, and shouting as a child shouts that it was his, that he had fought for it and would not give it up. And nothing answered him but laughter, of a kind that was very ugly to his ears because it was neither human nor amused nor even cruel. He looked up and all around to see where it came from, clutching his world tight, and there was a Being, lapped in darkness and veiled in clouds, a thing incongruously like a mountain with a great domed head. It looked at him, with no eyes that he could see, and the atoms that were in him began to move apart until his body was like a film of smoke and the world slipped through his ghostly fingers, and the Being took it, saying, "It is mine." Kirby woke before dawn, not very much rested.

Shari was awake, too. She said, "Let me go with you."

"No. I took you into the R-ship with me because I had to, but this is different."

"I might be able to warn you."

"I've had a warning. There'll be twenty-five of us; it can't surprise us all at once. And if we do have to fight or run, I don't want you there to worry about."

She glowered at him, half rebellious and half relieved. He smiled. "Besides, if you came, all the other wives would want to come too. Don't wish that on me!"

Reluctantly she nodded and went to get his breakfast. While he was eating it she disappeared, and did not return until the party was almost ready to go, twenty-four sleepy-eyed men loaded with three portable chainsaws that worked on atomic batteries, and a dozen old-fashioned axes. Kirby carried a long double-handed saw, two hatchets, and a shocker. He still wished he had a gun.

Shari shook her head and said in rapid Martian so the others would not understand, "I tried again, but there was nothing. Be careful, Kirby."

The other wives were waving their good-byes. You let somebody else cut down those trees, Joe; I don't want you anywhere near them when they fall, you hear me, Joe? Be awfully careful with that axe; you could cut your leg off and bleed to death up there; did anybody remember to take plenty of bandages and things? And watch out for wild animals, and I'll be just sick with worry every minute until you get back.

The men trudged off, convinced that not one of them could possibly survive.

But the sun rose and burned away the gloom for everybody but Kirby. He was at the head of the column. Wilson was beside him, carrying the field radio, and big George Krejewski, and Weiss the cyberneticist, and the curly-headed kid Marapese who had studied to be a pilot on the voyage and who had spent several years simultaneously worshipping Kirby and hoping that he would break his neck, not permanently, of course, so that he, Marapese, might land the *Lucy B. Davenport* as no ship had ever been landed before. Wilson, Weiss, Krejewski, and Kirby had fought the R-ship together and it made a sort of bond between them, but at this moment it gave Kirby the creeps. It seemed too coincidental to be healthy.

They followed the course of the tributary, and by the time the companion sun came up they had reached the limits of their geographic knowledge. Nobody had thought it wise to go exploring by twos and threes or alone, and there had been too much to do to spare men for big parties like this one. The true forest, where the big trees were, was still a good way off. Kirby expected to reach it in the late afternoon, but he figured to make camp along the stream and in the open. He wanted daylight before they went in among those mammoth trees.

There were tracks in the mud along the bank, where creatures had come down to drink. The hoofed ones seemed to be still in the odd-toed-ungulate stage, but there were others that showed a characteristic pad-and-claw pattern, and presently they came upon the remains of a carnivore's dinner. They looked at it for some time with the civilized townman's disgusted wonder at the messiness of primitive living and dying, and Kirby said, "No stragglers, please. The critter must have been the size of a lion to pull down a buck that big."

They saw one later in the afternoon, a thick yellowish animal barred and splashed with brown. It watched them from the edge of a thicket, and snarled, and then melted silently away.

That was all. A menace, perhaps, but a normal one, and not dangerous if they stayed together. Nothing came out of the forest. There was no sound but the wind, and the bird-things calling.

Nothing happened that night, either. They built a ring of fires and set guards, armed with the shockers that were powerful enough to stun anything within reason at close range. There was no occasion to use them. At dawn Kirby talked by radio with the ship, mustered his forces, and covered the remaining mile or so to the forest's edge.

It was virgin forest, such as had not been seen on Earth for centuries. The trees went up and up until their tops were lost and the craning onlooker toppled backward. The trunks were of a size that made the idea of cutting them with little saws and axes seem like mere folly. They were hoary-looking trees, hung over with vines and moss and waxy parasitical flowers and huge fungi. Often they bore their own dead upon their shoulders, where some giant had reeled over in a storm-wind and not found room to fall. To these men, city-born and city-bred on mechanized, urban worlds, it was overpowering and in an odd way deeply exciting. When their first awed reaction was over they began to finger their axes and look hungrily at the trunks.

Kirby strained his ears and heard nothing but the rustle of leaves far overhead, and the faint skitterings and skreekings of the small people who live in all woods and are no danger to anybody.

He talked to the ship again. "It looks okay. We'll start setting up a permanent camp, and the boys reckon to cut down the first tree today, just to see how it's done."

Fenner, the *Lucy's* operator on the other end, laughed and started to say something, and then the radio exploded into the wildest burst of static a man ever had to deafen his ears. Kirby said a startled word or two, and suddenly realized that Wilson was tugging at his sleeve. He was jabbing his other hand in the air, and shouting. Kirby turned off the radio and in the abrupt silence Wilson bellowed, ". . . over there quick, before—"

Kirby jumped up. He sprang forward two or three steps in the direction Wilson was pointing, and Wilson finished in a much smaller voice, ". . . before it's gone."

"Where?" said Kirby, getting his shocker in his hand.

"Right there. Well, it was there. I guess it's gone now."

Kirby and all the others quartered the whole area. There was nothing there, not even any tracks showing on the thick mat left by a million years of falling leaves.

Kirby said, "What was it, Wils?"

"I didn't get a good look. But it was big."

"As big as a dog, or a man, or an elephant? How big?"

"About so." Wilson indicated a height and width that called nothing readily to mind, except that it was wider than a man and shorter than an elephant. "It didn't make any noise. I just happened to see it out of the corner of my eye, like a darker shadow, and then before I could attract your attention it was gone again."

"Must be fast on its feet," said Marapese, with an insulting note of doubt. "Also light, not to make any noise with all these branches and twigs lying around." He walked about, crackling at every step.

"Stop it," said Kirby. "We don't know what might be in here, or what it can do. Let's not get too sure of ourselves." He went to the radio again. He felt very insecure and uneasy. The static had stopped. Fenner had hung on, waiting, and he got perhaps three sentences through to him before the thing blew again. "That's fine," said Kirby. "That is just dandy."

McLeod, a small rusty-haired man who knew radios better than he knew his own children, looked it over. "Nothing wrong here. Interference of some kind, but I can't imagine what. It worked all right this morning." He turned the dial, frowning, and got another blast of static."

"Yeah," said Kirby. "It worked out on the plain." And he thought, Supposing a Thing that can see inside atoms, that Thing would not have any trouble at all jamming a radio.

It suddenly became immensely important to talk to the ship again. "Mac, let's take it out there and try it. George you come along too. Let's make that a rule, never go anywhere except in threes. Keep your eyes open, and if you want to cut something down, pick a tree close to the water."

They had a book on Lumbering: How To Do It. He left them with it and went back with Mac and George Krejewski, out onto the plain. They kept the radio on, but throttled down so that the static did not deafen them. Two or three times Kirby thought he heard Fenner's voice, but the static kept on. Kirby's spine grew colder and his steps faster. Mac said, "What's put the wind up you? It's only static."

And then it was gone. It was gone entirely and the voice of Fenner came through clear as a bell, saying quite insanely, ". . . sure it'll repeat, it's taped of course and set to start broadcasting by some kind of mass-proximity device. Still very faint, but it won't stay that way and Kirby, if you don't clear up that damn static jam—oh. You're there. Stay there, don't go away again."

MacLeod said, "What the hell?"

Krejewski looked at Kirby, and Kirby said into the transmitter, "Fenner. Stop babbling. What is it?"

Fenner said, "I'm going to shift my mike. It's coming in again. Listen."

Crackle, crackle, pop, very faint, like an old-fashioned phonograph record with dust on it.

Then a voice, also very faint, a midget speaking down a tube you could measure in fractions of light-year. Speaking clearly and slowly, so that even an idiot child should understand.

"From the RSS-2 to the *Lucy B. Davenport*, a

100

corded message, Minor Howell, President of the United Worlds of the Solar System, to Captain Philip Kirby. Your data were incomplete. The full report of the RSS-1 showed an unidentified element present on Alpha Centauri III which makes it untenable for human life. I repeat, the planet is not habitable for humans. The RSS-2 is a converted carrier with all necessary supplies aboard to accommodate your entire company. The RSS-2 will make a single landing, and then return. For the sake of the women and children, I urge you to see that all your people return with it, as no further attempt can be made to rescue you. And I give you my personal assurance that no punitive action will be taken against you upon your return."

Crackle, scratch, click. And another voice.

"It is imperative that you broadcast your coordinates. RSS-2 cannot land unless your position is known. Broadcast your coordinates. Estimated landing time, 5 days, 14 hours, Solar Standard Time. This message will be repeated every hour."

Silence.

IX

ilence.

Fenner's voice came through it, thin and sharp with panic. "Did you hear that, Kirby? Did you hear what it said?"

Kirby said, "Yes, I heard." The sunlight was hot on the back of his neck. Under his feet were bruised grasses and a species of purple wildflower. They had a bittersweet, greenish smell. He did not feel anything much inside, except the automatic knotting up of the central ganglion. What were you supposed to feel at a moment like this?

Without knowing that he was going to do it, he shouted, "They couldn't let us alone, could they? All that distance away, but they couldn't let us alone!"

". . . did it mean?" Krejewski was saying. "What kind of an element? An element like uranium, or weather, or like 'elements of the Fleet,' or—" He let his voice fade out. It did not sound like his voice.

Unidentified element. Unidentified Thing that sees through atoms, that can comprehend in toto a mechanism so complex that it requires a team of experts to comprehend even its apparent parts. It had contact with RSS-1. And RSS-1 must have recorded it somewhere in the mass of information brought back from its voyage.

Untenable for human life. And so this was how i ended. This, after triumph, was the feel and the tast and the smell of defeat.

Fenner's voice, insistent, shrill. "Could that b true? We made all the tests and nothing showed up Could there be something here that our tests didn show?"

MacLeod said slowly, "Our data were incomplet Only a few top Government men ever saw the fu report, and only scraps of it were smuggled out. W just assumed—" He stared at Kirby, stricken wi guilt and fear. "All those women and kids. Kirb what have we done?"

Blind rage, violent, sudden, childishly denyi

reason. "I don't believe it! I would not believe the goddam Government on oath!"

But was it denying reason? There was a discrepancy here, a lack of logic. "Listen, they tried to kill us themselves, didn't they? They sent the RSS-1 after us with torpedoes, didn't they?"

There was only one answer to that. "Yes."

"All right. Now why are they suddenly so all-fired anxious to save our lives that they'd fit out another R-ship and sent it all the way out here to rescue us from an 'unidentified' danger? You answer me that."

They could not.

"Well, I can," Kirby said, rushing ahead as though by sheer savagery he could make the words be true. "It's a trap. Look, we broke the unbreakable law. We upset their whole system of government by proving that their R-ships weren't invincible, that men could still defy them and go anywhere they wanted to. They tried to kill us—a legal execution. It didn't work, and we proved to the Solar System that space was still free. But they can't let it stay proved or their whole concept of government will collapse. So they've tried a different way."

"You think," said Krejewski, "that the idea is to get us all together in this second R-ship and then blow it up or something?"

Kirby considered that. "I doubt it. It wouldn't be effective. Don't you get the picture? We left in an old manned rocket and a blaze of glory. We come back humbly in an R-ship, rescued by the kind Government from the consequences of our own folly. Now the Government is the hero and we're chumps, and all the restive souls who are at this moment trying to break out and follow us will have second thoughts, and nobody will ever try star-voyaging again, at least not in this era."

They thought that over, and the two suns blazed on Kirby's head and set a fire in it. When MacLeod said slowly, "It's your opinion, then, that the message is no more than a lie to frighten us into going home?", Kirby hesitated only a fractional second before he said, "Yes."

Damn the thing that can see inside of atoms. Damn it, and ignore it. It hasn't hurt anybody yet. Maybe it never will. And maybe Shari only dreamed it anyway.

"Fenner," he said into the radio. "Don't give our position, no matter how loud anybody screams at you. We're coming back."

"Fat lot of good that'll do," said Fenner sourly, and signed off. Kirby turned around. "Let's get the others," he said to MacLeod and Krejewski. He started back toward the forest. He was shaking and dizzy, and he walked fast because if he did not he would have to stop and be sick.

RSS-2. Robot Star Ship Two. They must, he thought, have worked overtime and Sundays to fit one up so fast. But they would. They would have to. They had had a complete monopoly on space for too long to let it be broken without a struggle by a bunch of undistinguished people like themselves. There must be millions of other undistinguished people who, like them, were tired of living like children constantly guarded and supervised for their own good. And if enough of them asserted their right to a universe with no manmade fences to close it off the present government and its policy of stagnation-for-profit—the government's profit through the trade and passenger monopoly of the robot ships—would be finished.

Perhaps enough people had already rebelled so that merely destroying the people of the *Lucy Davenport* was no longer enough. They had now to be discredited, and this was the way to do it.

And now, thought Kirby, I'm caught between two of them—another R-ship, and It, the mountain-without-a-face.

He said aloud, "They won't get away with it."

MacLeod and Krejewski stopped talking between themselves and looked at him.

"I'm going to find out," Kirby said.

"Find out what?" asked MacLeod.

"Whether this thing is dangerous to human life."

"What thing, though? That's the trouble. What, and where, and how do you go about finding it?"

They looked around them, and the world had grown enormous and far-spreading, and full of sinister mysteries.

They walked in among the trees to the place where they had left the others. A couple of them were chopping clumsily at a ten-foot-thick tree bole, not making much headway. In three different places, three separate groups of men were hunkered down around the three chainsaws, poking at them.

Kirby said bluntly, "Pack up. We've got to go back."

"Might as well," said a big man named Hanawalt. "We can't do much with the axes alone, we aren't good enough. And the chainsaws won't work."

"What do you mean, they won't work?" Krejew-ski demanded. "They worked all right day before yesterday. I tested them myself."

"They don't work now," said Hanawalt. "Nothing wrong with 'em. They just don't work."

"That's crazy."

"So," said MacLeod, "was the radio."

"We can worry about that later," Kirby said, and knocked radios and chainsaws out of their heads with the news of the oncoming R-ship. They took it first in a stunned silence, and then with such an out-burst of talk and questions, curses and speculation that Kirby had all he could do to get them loaded up and ready to move. And then the sound and the fury died away and there was only the quiet of dis-heartened and discouraged men.

"A hell of a thing," said Wilson. "All this way, all the years we put in."

"We're not licked yet," said Kirby, and swung the long saw over his shoulders again.

Wilson glanced at him and asked, "Aren't we?"

Kirby turned away from him. "Everybody ready?" They were lined up in a straggling line and their thoughts were plain on their faces. They were not good thoughts. Hanawalt muttered, "I hate to think what my wife is going to say to me."

Somebody else said, "We're all in the same boat." Which made it no better.

Kirby kicked irritably at a blanket roll and an axe left lying on the ground, and demanded to know who they belonged to. "No need to start throwing away good equipment just because you're scared."

A few of them answered him back rather nastily

and it developed that the blanket roll did not belong to anybody. Each man had his full load.

The feeling of sickness in Kirby's middle became almost unbearable. He asked, "Who's missing?"

After a moment or two, they came up with a name. "Joe Marapese."

"Oh, lord," said Kirby. "All right, let's find him."

They fanned out, yelling, working in a widening circle until Kirby was afraid they would get out of touch with each other and he pulled them in, lest he lose some more. There was no Joe Marapese. There was no blood, no sign of a struggle, no tracks, human or otherwise. There had not been, that anyone could remember, even the smallest sound.

"Wandered off exploring," Kirby said. He repeated it with a harsh note of firmness. "We can't wait all day for him." He scribbled a note and left it on Marapese's blanket. "He can catch up with us."

The others did not look happy about it, but they did not protest. All at once they seemed very anxious to get out of the forest. Kirby did not try to hold them back.

The plain was wide and empty. They plodded across it, not talking much. First one sun went down, and then the other, and they went on through the twilight and into darkness. It was Kirby who first saw the black hull of the *Lucy B. Davenport* against the sky, with the circle of fires around her base like a winkling mockery of stars. And he thought, They're mine, these people. I brought them here, and I won't let them go. I won't let it all be made for nothing!

Then in a few minutes, when they were closer,

the wives of the men came running out to meet them, and Kirby thought, this time I won't have much to say about it.

He left them to look for Shari. She was waiting, as she always did, apart from the others. Even in the dusk outside the firelight her face looked strained, and when she took his hands her fingers were cold, holding his too tightly.

He nodded toward the women. "Have they been like that all day?"

"Yes. But this morning, when they first heard the message—oh, Kirby! It was as if they all sat in a courtroom and heard the death sentence pronounced on them and everyone they love. They have locked up all the children in the ship, because they think now this world is somehow poisoned."

"That's what's going to beat us," said Kirby somberly. "Panic. The Government counted on that, of course. Men and women may be brave about their lives, but not the lives of their mates and especiall[y] not their children. That's the Government's majo[r] weapon, and I don't think they'll need another one Shari, we lost a man today."

She looked at him, startled. "Not killed? I trie[d] to follow you, but there were so many minds, s[o] many emotions—"

"He just disappeared. Young Marapese. Shari, wi[ll] you see if you can find him? I want to know if he[']s still alive."

Marapese's folks would be interested in knowin[g] too.

Shari walked away from the fires, out into th[e] darkness, away from the people. She said, "Y[ou] should have taken me with you. I could only get confusion of things. It was thinking toward you this time, not toward the ship. What did it do?"

"Jammed the radio. Stopped the chainsaws from working, and don't ask me how, but there's no other explanation. Now I want to know—did it take young Marapese?"

"I'll try." She shut her eyes and was silent for several minutes. Then she said, "I cannot hear him. If he is alive, he is very far away."

He asked her, "Is the message true?"

She answered, as he had known she would, "I do not know."

"I want to find out. I'd like your help, Shari, but this time you don't have to give it. This time the R-ship is coming, not to kill you, but to take you back. You have a free choice."

She made a small sound that might have been laughter, except that it was a little too sharply barbed. "Where you are concerned, my choice is never free."

"I tried to make you stay at home."

"And I came. And I will help."

He put his arm around her and walked with her back to the ship. The people had fallen quiet, except for a few hushed sobs. And then, high and unearthly, a woman shrieked.

"There's a light on the plain—*something's out here!*"

X

There was a confusion of screams and cries, and then, as though a great gust of wind had picked them up like grains of dust, the people moved all together toward the ship's main hatch. Kirby grabbed Shari back out of the way, yelling as loud as he could at them to keep their heads. Some of the men were trying to stem the rush but it was not doing any good. The mob streamed up the ramp, jammed and squeezed and popped like corks in through the hatchway, and were gone.

Pop Barstow came out from under the ramp where he had taken refuge, and a minute or two later three men and then a couple more came back out of the hatch, looking sheepish.

Pop Barstow chuckled. "Didn't know they could move so fast, did you, Kirby?" He added, "They're real bugged by that message, and I got to admit so am I. The worst of it's not knowing what the danger is."

Krejewski was among the men, and Wilson. They came up to Kirby. "Did you see the light?"

"No. But we better look for it. Got your shockers?"

They went together through the circle of fires, into the outer night. Shari did not move, standing with her eyes shut. Suddenly she cried out,

"Kirby, wait!"

She ran after them between the fires. Kirby caught her. He pointed out into the black void. A beam

110

light showed. It shot up strongly from the ground, and then wavered erratically, and fell. It seemed to be about a quarter of a mile away. The men swore uneasily. Wilson said, "What do you suppose that is?"

Shari said, "It's Marapese."

Kirby stared down at her in the darkness. "What? But a minute ago—"

"A minute ago he was not there. Now he is."

"Marapese," said Wilson. He looked in the direction of the light, and then in the direction of the forest where they had last seen him. "How did he get there?"

"Well," said Kirby, "let's go get him." He patted Shari. "Go on back to the ship and tell 'em. That'll quiet them down."

Shari said acidly, "I doubt if they will believe me, but I'll try."

Kirby and the others went out across the plain. They had pocket torches, but even so they stumbled heavily in the tangled grasses and the clumps of sturdy weed. The distant light flared up again, and again was lost.

Krejewski said, "He's using his torch to signal. He must be hurt or something. Why didn't he just walk the rest of the way?"

They speculated uselessly on the whys and wherefores of Marapese's condition. The light was farther off than they had thought, but presently they came up to it. It was Marapese. He was sitting down holding the torch between his hands and then dropping it in a peculiarly childish way, as though he kept forgetting what he was doing with it. He let out a wild yell when the men came up, and then he stared

111

at Kirby and the others as though he couldn't remember who they were. He did not seem to be hurt. His clothing was muddy and his hair was wet, but beyond that he was all right, at least physically.

Kirby knelt down beside him. "Joe." he said. "It's me, Kirby. Joe, look here."

Joe looked. Then he began to cry.

Kirby shook him. "Stop that. Shut it up."

Marapese's teeth came together with an audible clack. "I'm cold," he said. "I'm all wet."

Kirby looked at his own hands. He had used them to shake the boy, and there was mud on them, still fresh. "Where'd you get this?" he asked Marapese. "What happened to you?"

"I don't know."

Something quivered inside Kirby. He had heard Shari use those same words too often. "Look," he said. "You wandered away from us in the woods. You went somewhere. Where?"

"I didn't," said Marapese, and made a series of unpleasant hic-ing sounds in his throat. Kirby shook him again.

"Come on, now. Tell me about it."

"I didn't go anywhere! I just went for one minute behind a tree, and I wasn't ten feet away from Wils and Hanawalt. They were trying to get one of the chainsaws going. And I wasn't there any more."

"What do you mean, you weren't there any more?"

"I was in another place, that's what I mean! One minute I was behind the tree, and the next minute there wasn't any tree and I was up to my knees in water in a damned great swamp, and none of the guys were around."

Wilson snorted. Marapese had not believed in his animal, and he was not going to believe Marapese's miraculous translation in space. "You wandered off like a idiot and fell in a bog, that's all."

But Kirby, who was cold all through now with an icy chill that was not borne on any wind, fingered the wet mud on his palm and asked, "How did you get here, Joe? Did you walk?"

"No," said Marapese. "I just . . . came."

"Like it happened before? You were there, and then you were here, just like that?"

"Yeah."

"You didn't black out any time?"

"No. I wandered around the swamp all day, trying to find my way out. I couldn't figure it, and I was scared, but I didn't black out. Then it got dark."

He lapsed into a violent fit of shivering, and when he spoke again his words were punctuated by the chattering of his teeth.

"Then I was really scared. I thought I was going to die there and nobody would ever find me. I kept wallowing around, falling over things, and then here I was."

His voice went up a couple of octaves, until it sounded like a girl's. "Look, if you don't believe me, my clothes are still wet. Look at my boots. I didn't get all that gunk on them walking across a dry plain."

"You know," said Krejewski on a note of pure awe, "that's true."

They looked out into the great dark, and Wilson muttered, "First the radio, and then the saws, and now this, and you can't explain any of them."

Kirby said bitterly, "*Ad astra per ardua*, remember? Well, we've had the *ardua*, plenty of it, more than enough. It isn't fair!" he shouted, out into the night, out toward the forest and the far-off peaks. "It isn't fair, damn you!"

He started to haul Marapese to his feet, not gently at all but roughly and cursing while he did it in a fumbling sort of way, not picking his words well. "You can't fight everything. It was hard enough to get here—we had a right to some breaks."

Krejewski came up on the other side of Marapese. "Okay, Kirby, I'll give you a hand."

They slogged back over the plain, half leading, half carrying Marapese, whose clothes were drying on him fast now in the wind, as though to bear him out. Kirby had stopped cursing. His teeth were shut tight together and he put each foot down hard, stamp, and then stamp again, as though he were marching someplace to a driving music no one else could hear. After a long while he asked Marapese a question.

"Where was this swampy place?"

"I don't know. Somewhere in the forest, I guess. It felt like a long way off."

"See anything there?"

"Trees, all dead. Mud and water and reeds."

"Anything else? Anything alive?"

Marapese did not answer.

"Well, did you?"

"I didn't see anything. But I thought I heard things moving around, and some of the things I fell over."

He began to cry again, dismally, like a frightened child.

"They weren't there, Kirby. I'd stumble, and then whatever in heaven it was would be gone."

The night was huge and dark, and the wind blew wide over the prairie. The men began to walk very fast toward the fires, dragging Marapese with them.

Most of the people were still inside the ship. They got Marapese down to the cargo deck, where his family took him over in a setting of tired pandemonium. Nobody, apparently, had any thought of sleep. Children cried, and there was a noise of talking as incessant as the sound of running water. It did not abate as the men told the story of Marapese.

Kirby took Shari outside into the corridor and told it to her. "It sounds like something I've read or heard about," he said. "Something with a name."

She gave him a Martian word that meant something like "thought-moving", and he said, "Teleportation. That's it. Well, I suppose if you can see atomic structure, moving things around wouldn't be too difficult." He shivered. "I sometimes think the crackpots were right and God never meant us to make the stars. Everything's against us. R-ships, and now super-beings with a psi power as big as all outdoors. How are you going to fight that?"

From the open hatch came the sound of a woman's voice crying out to somebody, ". . . brought us here without knowing whether this world was safe or not!"

A man's voice answered miserably, "We thought we knew. There was nothing to make us doubt it."

"You thought you knew," the woman repeated slowly. "Oh, my God."

Wilson stuck his head through the hatch and said to Kirby, "I think you better come down."

Wearily Kirby did so. They had been ripening for trouble all day, and Marapese's weird adventure was the final push. Out of the crowd somebody said angrily,

"Fenner says you told him not to broadcast our position to the R-ship."

"That's right," Kirby said. "I did."

There was a muted sort of howl, and Sally Wilson's voice rang out clearly, "You're not giving the orders any more. We'll make up our own minds this time, whether we want to live or die."

"I only thought," said Kirby, with a mildness he did not feel, "that the position should not be given until everybody had had a chance to think about it." He climbed up the ladder a few rungs and tried to get the attention of the whole group. "Will you quiet down and listen to me for a minute? This is the biggest decision you'll ever make in your lives. Don't make it too hastily. The R-ship—"

"Decision!" somebody cried. "Does anybody have to think twice before they decide to save their children from a horrible death—if it isn't already too late?"

"Nobody," said Kirby, "is asking you to stay and face death. It just seems like an elementary piece of common sense to find out if we actually are facing death before we lie down and quit. We can give the R-ship our position any time up to a day before it's due to land, but once we do give it, that's it. We'll have the R-ship whether we want it or not, and it might not be so easy to get rid of."

Wilson said, "A couple of times today you talked as though you knew something, Kirby. Do you? Have you got a line on this 'unidentified element'?"

"Shari has."

"Well," said somebody nastily, "that makes it all different." In the brisk round of comment that followed Kirby discovered what he had not known before, that many of the women were jealous of Shari's power, and refused to believe in it, while others were not jealous at all but simply did not believe in it, or else felt that it was far too chancy a thing to trust.

There was a further point of view. "And of course Shari wouldn't dream of lying just to make *you* look good."

"I don't think she would," said Kirby. "After all, she likes living too." To Wilson he said, "There's another point. It's always been accepted that the RSS-1's report was not made public because it showed a habitable world out here and people might be tempted to try and get to it. Well, if the report showed it wasn't habitable, why not publish it, with the films and everything for proof, and settle the matter once and for all?"

"I hadn't thought of that," said Wilson. "It does seem they would have, all right. And yet there is something on this world, Kirby. It might be something—" He hesitated, and then finished. "Well, something the cameras couldn't photograph."

Mountain-without-a-face, thought Kirby, harking back to the symbolic figure of his dream. It could be without a body, too. Marapese had not seen anything.

With sullen stubbornness, he said, "I'm going to y and find out, anyway, before I throw away a ide new world just because Minor Howell doesn't ant me to have it."

A small plump woman with a small plump jaw

117

like a steel trap elbowed her way to the front. She was Fenner's wife, and she had been a radio operator herself in Civil Communications before her marriage. Kirby's heart had begun to sink before she ever opened her mouth.

"All this arguing," she said, "is beside the point. Nobody else had guts enough to take the responsibility, but I did. I broadcast the coordinates."

XI

One by one, on the heels of Mrs. Fenner's statement, the people in the cargo deck stopped talking. It got so still that the sniffling of the children and the occasional creaking of a cot as somebody moved on it were almost painfully loud.

That was it. The decision made and finished. After a full day of emotional debauch, it was as sobering as a slap in the face.

It had a strange effect on Kirby. A single surge of intense anger died away almost before it was formed, and he remembered, as he stood there on the ladder looking out over the crowded deck, how he had stood there once before when the ship was in deep space and how his own courage had run out of him under the weight of that responsibility.

Now he saw Mrs. Fenner's two small children huddled together on their cot, not understanding what all the uproar was about but scared to death by it and Fenner himself trying to comfort them, and he said to the defiant woman with the fear in her eyes "I guess in your place I'd have done the same thing."

It was odd that he had never felt that protective anguish about Shari. He wondered whether it was some lack in his own emotional equipment, or whether it was because Shari always seemed so surely in control of her own mind and actions that it was impossible to think of her as helpless in any sense of the word.

Fenner glanced up at Kirby and then away again. "I couldn't stop her," he said. "She waited until I went out. I didn't know it till afterward."

"Somebody was bound to do it," Kirby said.

"But she didn't have any right to take it on her self!" someone cried shrilly from the back of the crowd. "It was for all of us to decide!"

There was a chorus of assent, quite loud.

Mrs. Fenner's tight little jaw sagged down in honest astonishment. "But that's what you wanted!"

"It wasn't up to you to do it," said the same voice, and then the owner of it began to cry. "I just can't face another five years out there cooped up in a damned old ship again!"

A second chorus, even louder.

Mrs. Fenner turned, oddly enough, to Kirby, saying, "But they did want it."

Kirby refrained from making the obvious comment on the difficulty of decision. He only said, "No, they didn't really. You see, they don't want either to go or to stay."

He started to climb the ladder. Wilson caught him.

"Wait, Kirby. Do you think there is a chance?"

Kirby shrugged.

"We still have a little time," Wilson said. "Let's find out. I don't want to go back unless I have to."

119

Krejewski came up, and Weiss. "That's right. And if we find out the message is a lie, we can just tell the R-ship to take off again."

"Like old times," said Kirby. "No, you guys have done enough. Stick with the wife and kids."

"Weiss said, "This is our world too, Kirby. "You can't have all the glory."

"Yeah," said Hanawalt, shoving his way to the ladder. "Suppose you got hurt or something; what would happen to Shari? You can't go alone. And anyway, like Weiss says—"

Suddenly every man in the place was demanding to go.

"I'll be damned," said Kirby. "Okay. But four will be enough. Wilson, Weiss, Krejewski, Hanawalt. You yelled the loudest. Don't blame me."

He went up the ladder, moving like a high-school boy, as though he had never been tired in his life. He took hold of Shari and hugged her.

"Humans," he said. "They're crazy. Absolutely crazy. Let's get some sleep."

They started before the first dawn, when the air was dim and cool and sweet, and it did not seem possible that there could be danger anywhere in the world. They carried every piece of equipment they could think of that might be helpful and would not weigh them down, and they were a curiously grim little expedition. The send-off they got was on the grim side, too, reflecting the confusion of desires that had turned the ship's company from a cohesive whole into merely a lot of people.

Pop Barstow wished them luck, and then got Kirby off to one side for a minute. "What happen if we don't hear from you before the R-ship lands?"

"You will."

"But if we don't?"

"You'll have to make up your own minds, go or stay."

"Every man for himself," Pop said. "Yeah. Only you know how that turns out. If one family goes they all go. Kirby—"

"Yeah."

"You're a stubborn man, young Kirby. An onery one, too. I just want to ask you, do you believe in what you're doing, or are you risking five other necks besides your own, including your wife's, because you won't give up?"

Kirby looked at the old man, and then at the ground. "I wish you hadn't asked me that, Pop," he said. "Because honest to God, I can't answer it."

He rejoined the others and they went off, following the same route along the watercourse that they had taken on the ill-starred lumbering expedition. The spot in the forest from which Marapese had disappeared seemed to be the logical starting point, if there was any logical starting point.

"Well," said Weiss to Shari, "what do we look for? Intelligent crystals, globes of force, ten-foot lobster men, invisible monsters?" He was trying to be funny, but it did not come off. Shari shook her head.

"I know no more than you." She walked along for a time, very thoughtful, looking away at the forest. "It is strange that I can never get a conscious thought from this source—I mean, an ordinary thought. It must keep its mind well guarded. Unless—"

"Unless," said Weiss, "its mental processes are so alien that your mind can't recognize them at all;

121

unless there's a specific projection like the one of the R-ship's brain that you can fit into your frame of reference."

"You sound like a psychologist," Kirby said.

"A cyberneticist," Weiss said stiffly, "is much the same thing. Only we do it with an electron here and a transistor there. A machine can think faster and remember more things than a man, and it can perform more functions simultaneously. It is unfailingly accurate, granting that its information is accurate, of course. But even a machine has to have a frame of reference, or the information fed to it is meaningless."

"Then you mean," said Kirby, "that It could be thinking away there somewhere and Shari wouldn't be able to get it at all?"

"Even psi powers have their limitations, Kirby. They're not supernatural."

Looking at the forest, Kirby grunted, "These are."

"No," said Weiss. "Not in that sense. They may be completely alien and unknown to us, but they still are bound by natural law and operating within their own logical framework."

"Sure," said Kirby. "Theoretically. But practically speaking, is that going to help us much?"

"Probably," Weiss admitted, "not much."

They tramped along, sometimes silent, sometimes speculating or questioning Shari over and over until she was weary of repeating. The day was perfect of its kind, a segment of full summer with two suns to blaze in the sky and a wind running hot and dry across a thousand miles of prairie to burn their face a deeper brown. A fine day, a fine country. But emotionally they walked through it in a vacuum, hold

122

ing everything in abeyance. It was not the time yet for hope, for fear, for anything. It was the time for walking, and they walked.

In the afternoon a storm blew up from the south-west. They sweated it out crouched under their tarps, and after it was over they wallowed on through the mud to make a camp where they had stopped before, clear of the forest. Damp and tired, they huddled around a hopeless little fire and chewed a cold supper. And now for the first time they had a definite feeling about the expedition.

"What's the use? How can you find something when you don't even know what you're looking for or where it is?"

Krejewski said it, and it was shocking to Kirby that it should be so, because Krejewski had always been solid, stolid, cheerful, and matter-of-fact about everything. And because he felt exactly the same way, Kirby said with unnecessary viciousness, "You can go back in the morning, if you want to. You know where the ship is."

A quarrel started then, and they all got into it, snapping wearily at each other until Shari broke it up. Then, as they rolled up in their blankets, Weiss said,

"If I could only figure out why it wanted to con-tact the R-ship. That's the key to the business right there. Why had it perceived and remembered, down to the last atom, the cybernetic control-center of the R-ship?"

Hanawalt answered, "It seems to be interested in mechanisms. Remember the chainsaws? I'll bet it has picture of them, too. Incidentally, they worked all ight again back at the ship."

"Then it—" Weiss hesitated, then blurted out, "It must have damped the atomic batteries."

"Mentally?"

"How else?"

"God," said Hanawalt. "Well, anyway, it didn't kill Marapese." He stressed the word "kill" heavily and hopefully.

"Perhaps," said Kirby, "It just wanted to look. It's never seen humans before."

Wilson said uneasily, "It didn't seem to like him very well, the way it shot him back. Maybe the next time—"

"It is possible," said Shari, drowning him out, "that we have one advantage. If Its mind is closed to me, perhaps It can't understand our thoughts, either."

"Frame of reference," Weiss pointed out triumphantly. "That's what I said."

Presently they slept, and Kirby dreamed again about the mountain-without-a-face. Only it was different this time, more crudely anthropoid, less symbolic. This time it had hands. It picked up the tiny human figures one by one and examined them and threw them away. It picked up Kirby and lifted him into the air, screaming with terror of the height and the wind that blew there, and it looked into him out of the great muffled darkness of its face until his flesh began to separate from itself most unpleasantly. Then it tossed him away and he fell and fell and fell until Shari shook him awake to stop his yelling and it was dawn and time to eat and go on again into the forest.

"Maybe we ought to hold off," Wilson said, "u[n]

til we think up some kind of a plan. I mean, what are we going to do when we get there?"

"If I knew," Kirby said, "the chances are I wouldn't go in there at all. And if you can think of a plan, fine. But I don't think we can afford to wait for it."

He looked upward, where somewhere beyond the sky the RSS-2 rushed swift and unswerving toward them.

They loaded themselves and started on, in bright new sunshine that steamed the moisture out of the ground and the cold out of their bones. They would have felt good about it, except that every step brought them closer to the forest, and the trees looked higher and darker and less welcoming by the minute.

Kirby halted at the last possible rim, where the sunlight stopped and the shadows took over. He looked at Shari.

She shook her head. "Nothing."

With the feeling of a man who jumps off a very high cliff into unknown waters, Kirby said, "Let's go."

XII

The forest had not changed since the last time they saw it. The trees rocked gently, high up, in a breeze they could not feel, and it was all hushed and solemn and self-contained, owing nothing to the mind or the hands of man.

And somewhere in it, hidden away in the very

many miles of woods that spread along the flanks of the mountain range up to the timberline and down again to the verge of the prairie, something waited.

They had an instinctive desire to go softly and not attract anybody's attention. But the litter of fallen twigs and branches trapped their clumsy feet until it sounded to Kirby like a herd of cattle crashing along. He swore at the others, or started to, and then he realized that it did not make any difference. *It* did not have to hear them to know they were there. And anyway, they were here to find the thing, not hide from it. Crash away. Shout, whistle, and sing. The sooner the better. The sooner it's over, the sooner to—

To what?

To life? Death? Freedom? Or the R-ship and the long voyage home, because in their own persons the utter negation of what they had risked so much to prove.

You, thought Kirby, you faceless thing in the shadows, you stumbling block, watch out. Man has trampled down better things than you on his way over the mountains—gods and kings, parents and children, cities, nations, races, planets. Who are you to hold us back?

Fine words, murmured the restless trees. Fine words. But before you can trample you must find, and the days are short, and the speed of the R-ship is very great.

They came to the place where they had been before, with the futile axe-marks white on the one great dark bole, and the memory of fear clinging thick in the shadows.

"Stick close," said Kirby, quite unnecessarily, be-

126

cause they were already treading on one another's feet. "Shari, can't you hear anything yet?"

"The forest is full of voices, but they are all animal. They do not speak thoughts."

Quite unjustifiably, Kirby accused her of not trying. "It reached us here before, strong enough."

"I am doing my best," she answered, on a note of controlled fury he had never heard her use before.

"All right, all right, I'm sorry. I guess we'll have to wait."

They waited. Shari sat cross-legged on the ground. Her eyes were closed and she was frowning.

Nothing happened.

Shari's frown became deeper, the lines of her body more tense. The men sat down too, close together. Alternately they watched Shari and the spaces under the trees around them.

Time passed.

Nothing happened.

Shari groaned and lay back flat on the matted leaves. She said, "I'm tired."

Kirby patted her. "Get some rest. You can try again later."

"I don't understand it," she said. "The whole forest is watching us. Many, many creatures—oh, little creatures, Kirby, nothing to be afraid of. Some are alarmed, and some only curious, but none of them *think*. I can't touch any intelligence."

She rolled over, hiding her face in her arms. "It's no good. The thing's mind is too well guarded. I have not the skill nor the strength to break that barrier."

Kirby looked across her at the others. Hanawalt said, "Well, it was a good try. Now what?"

"Look for the swamp, I guess."

"The swamp?" said Krejewski. "Why?"

"Well, it took Marapese there, didn't it? That must be where it holds out. There, or close to it."

"Marapese didn't see anything."

"It must have hidden from him. Or maybe it's something he wouldn't recognize as being alive if he did see it." Kirby picked up bits of twig and threw them down again one by one into the mat of leaves. "Besides, remember what he said about falling over things, and then they weren't there? Doesn't that sound like teleportation? It must have been close by, playing with him."

They thought about that. Finally Wilson said, "Yeah, but even so, how are we going to find that swamp? It could be anywhere."

"Well," said Kirby, "I figure—"

"Look," said Wilson, "I'll lay it on the line. I asked to come here, didn't I? I wanted to find this thing just as much as you, didn't I? And we figured Shari could do it. Okay. So it didn't turn out that way, and I've got a wife and kids to think of. I'm not going to go blundering around in this forest looking for somethig that may be a hundred miles away, and maybe not be able to find my way back in time. If Sally and the kids go aboard that ship, I'm going to be there, too."

Kirby nodded slowly. He looked from Wilson to Krejewski and Hanawalt and Weiss. "I guess you felt the same way."

Weiss stared uncomfortably at the ground. "If there was more time, or we had any idea where the place was—"

"After all," Hanawalt said, "you know how you'd feel if Shari was back there waiting."

"Sure," said Kirby. He got up and went away from them between the trees. When he was out of sight he sat down again and put his head in his hands. He heard them calling after him but he did not answer. He was not angry with them. He did not blame them in the slightest. He simply did not want to be around them for a while.

He sat there for a long time, not thinking about anything in particular, feeling low and beyond caring any more. The shadows shifted as the twin suns climbed higher in the sky. It was hot, with the breathless unstirring heat of deep woods on a summer day. After a while the pangs of hunger began to nag him. Oh hell, he thought, what's the use? He got up and started back to join the others, and he had not taken more than half a dozen steps when he heard Wilson give a yelp like a schoolgirl who finds a mouse in her slipper. A shocker cracked, and then two more, very briefly. Then there was nothing but a confusion of voices, out of which emerged Krejewski's bull bellow, shouting Kirby's name.

Kirby began to run.

They were all standing together, looking wildly around. Perhaps six feet away a long unpleasant thing that had not been able to decide whether to be a lizard or a snake lay flapping its jaws and squirming feebly. Hanawalt was still pointing his shocker at it and futilely pressing the stud.

"It won't work," he said.

"None of them will. Kirby, It's found us! The minute we used the shockers on that brute—" Wilson

129

waved his own inoperative weapon under Kirby's nose. "It stopped them."

"All right," said Wilson, pointing. "It crawled right up on my foot before I saw it."

"Did Shari—" Kirby stopped suddenly. "Where is Shari?"

"Right here. At least she was a minute ago. When It stopped the shockers she kind of groaned, and then she ran off a little bit that way, northwest. She said that's where the thing was. She didn't go far, only a step or two. She's right here."

Kirby took a step or two that way himself, and then a lot more steps, shouting, calling, tearing into the shadows and the thorny fastnesses of windfalls. Once he thought he saw something peering at him through a curtain of vines but when he got there there was nothing.

And Shari was gone.

"Just like Marapese," said Weiss. He shivered, and Wilson said quickly,

"He wasn't hurt, Kirby. He got back all right."

"Yeah," said Kirby. "Sure." He stood still with his hands clenched and all the color ran out of his face under the brown burn so it looked like a piece of dead wood. And he was thinking about a lot of things, about Shari saying, "Where you are concerned my choice is never free," and about Pop Barstow asking him a question he could not answer.

The others watched, shocked and silent, afraid to speak to him, as though it were somehow their fault that this had happened.

Kirby said, "Go back to the ship. I don't want you on my conscience too."

He started to pick up the things he had laid aside. His fingers shook like an old man's.

"What are you going to do?" asked Wilson.

"Find her."

"We'll go with you."

"Get back to your families," Kirby said fiercely. "Tell Pop he was right. Go home."

He went away in the direction Shari had gone, northwest, half running, ripping and floundering by main strength through curtains of hanging vines and occasional patches of undergrowth. The others looked after him for a minute, and then at each other. Wilson muttered, "Maybe it's not too far. Another day won't matter."

They followed Kirby.

Kirby neither knew nor cared. He went on his way like a charging bull until he could not go any farther, and then he sat for a while on the ground, his head bent over his knees and his flanks heaving. After that he took it slower, but he did not stop again until it got dark and he fell over a big branch into a drift of leaves and just stayed there. The others, searching carefully with their lights along his trail, came up with him about an hour later and built a fire, roused him enough to get some food in him. He was up before daybreak and gone again. And again they followed, lagging even farther behind because now Kirby had got his second wind and was going at a pace that was steady but fast, so that only a driven man could keep up with it.

The long hot day drew on to another night, and there was no swamp and no sign of Shari.

Over the campfire Wilson said, "She may be back the ship by now. Like Marapese."

131

"Maybe," Kirby said.

"Look, we've got to start back in the morning."

"I told you to go in the first place."

"But we can't leave you alone up here, Kirby. It wouldn't be right."

"Go on," said Kirby. "Thanks. You're good friends. But I told you, go on."

He went to sleep, and so did they. In the morning he was gone, and this time they did not follow but turned their faces reluctantly toward the plain.

"If Shari's there when we get back," said Hanawalt, "we can let him know by radio. We ought to be able to get that much of a message through." Kirby was still carrying his light pack with the portable field radio.

"Sure," said Krejewski. "Or maybe he'll find her soon and they can catch up with us."

"Sure," said Krejewski. "He'll be okay."

"Hell," said Weiss. "What a fine bunch of liars we are."

Kirby had ceased to think about them. He was already miles away, moving in as straight a line as he could make it by compass, angling in toward the foothill slopes of a great saddle peak. He was not clearly aware of anything except the need to keep going toward Shari. He kept her name and his thoughts about her clear on the top of his mind so that if she was still alive she might hear them and know that he was coming. Twice, with a sort of animal cunning, he used his shocker in the hopes that It might teleport him too if he attracted Its attention. But all It did was damp the current in the shocker and ignore him.

132

He spent that night alone, lying where he happened to be when darkness overtook him.

He had neither food nor fire. It was not that he was too tired or distraught to bother. He simply did not think of them. He slept like a dead man, without dreams, and was away again with the first gray gleam of morning. The forest seemed queer and misty. He thought vaguely that the mist would clear as the sun rose, but it did not, and after a while he realized that he was carrying the mist with him, inside his head. Distances became uncertain. Sometimes a tree that seemed no more than twenty feet away would take him half an hour to get to. He tested his mind frequently to make sure it was still functioning clearly, reciting whole passages of the Spaceman's Manual and the Laws of Astrogation. As long as he could remember those, he knew he was all right.

What he did not know was that he had reached the borders of the swamp.

It was not until he fell down that he noticed that. He was used to falling down and it did not bother him anymore, but this time he went headfirst into a slough of muddy water. The shock was startling. He scrambled up, shaking his head and gasping, and some of his wits fell back into their proper places. Cautiously he looked around.

There was a low piece of land close by, with a huge dead tree on it shooting up stark and white, dangling fringes of pale moss from what was left of its limbs. Shari was standing beside it, looking at him. She had something in her arms.

"Shari," he whispered, and then shut his eyes.

133

When he opened them she was still there. He started to shout and run toward her, making a mighty churning of the water, and she held up one hand and said, "Softly, softly! Oh, Kirby, be careful!"

She was muddy, as Marapese had been, from head to foot, and her face showed chalk white where the streaks did not cover it. The thing in her arms was muddy, too. It moved and she stroked it. "Oh, Kirby," she murmured, and then she sat down carefully on the muddy ground and began to cry.

Kirby moved toward her, not speaking nor making any more noise than he could help. He got out of the water and crouched down in front of her. The thing she was holding gurgled and snorted in a contented, infantile way.

"Beloved," said Shari, no louder than a whisper. "how I have waited for you!" And the thing thrust out a moist little snout and nuzzled Kirby's hand.

XIII

"What—" Kirby started to ask.

Shari said softly, "Don't frighten her or she'll 'por you away."

"That?" said Kirby.

Shari nodded with complete solemnity.

Sitting still as a rock, Kirby stared at Shari an then at the fat, pinkish, lubberly creature in h arms, the four-footed and utterly animal creatu with the expression of happy imbecility. He tri several times, and finally the words came out, ca fully subdued.

"Are you trying to tell me that this is the thing we—"

"Yes."

"But it's only a baby. Isn't it?"

"Yes. But she can do as much as an adult, except that her range is short and her power not so great. Kirby, the thing we were looking for is not a single individual, it's a breed, a herd, a whole species. They're absolutely unbelievable."

It occurred to Kirby then to ask Shari if she was all right. And she began to cry again. "I followed you all the way here, beloved, with my mind, and I tried so hard to make you hear me."

"If you are all right, it doesn't matter." Kirby meant it. Nothing mattered. Not stars nor colonies nor R-ships. "What happens if I—"

"Gently, and I'll think her happy thoughts, and she'll love it."

Kirby took Shari and the pinkish creature into his arms and held them both in a muddy embrace, and that was when it all come over him, the aftermath of the days and nights when he had thought he would probably never see her again. It got dark, and through the darkness he could hear the creature gurgling. He began to laugh, and Shari began to laugh, and in a minute or two the darkness cleared. Kirby said, "You're all right, really?" And she answered, "At first I was terrified. And then I began to understand. After that, it was just making friends and waiting for you."

Kirby sat back on the mud. "I don't understand it all," he said. "To me she just looks moronic."

"She is."

"But—"

"They are. The whole species. That is why I could not find the intelligence I was searching for. There is none. The espees do not—"

"The what?"

"I suppose I have been calling them that in my mind, since ESP is their distinguishing characteristic. Whatever you call them, they do not think. They only feel."

"But they can see inside of atoms."

Rather impatiently Shari said, "All animals can see the world they live in. They do not necessarily understand it. Do you suppose a bird knows or cares what makes a tree grow, or that those hoofed ones out there on the prairie comprehend the wind or the shining of the suns?"

"No," said Kirby, "I guess not. But—"

"But these see farther than the others, that's all." Shari stroked the small espee and made her kick her fat legs with pleasure. "I think it is one of Mother Nature's mistakes on this world. She has not yet managed to evolve an intelligent species, but she has tried, and this is one of her efforts. She experimented with a psi mutation, but whether she chose the wrong physical form to put it into or whether the psi power itself stopped mental development by removing the need for it—if you can fell a tree by thinking about it, why invent the axe?—it was a complete dead end."

She rose. "Come, I'll show you. Walk quietly, and above all don't use any mechanism. They're sensitive to any release of energy and it frightens them. As soon as Marapese used his power-torch, they sent him away. They're very timid."

Still not believing it, Kirby said, "Is that why the

damped the atomic batteries and stopped radio transmission?"

"Yes. Their reflexes—"

The infant espee vanished cleanly from her arms in the middle of a grunt.

". . . are very simple," she finished.

"Simple," said Kirby. "Oh, yes. Very."

They walked, sinking in the mud, wading in shallow water. It was quiet and hot, and the shafts of dead trees stood up like the white pillars of some long-forgotten temple, hung with votive offerings of moss.

"It must have been one of them that Wilson saw. Teleported, of course. That's why it didn't make any noise coming or going. I guess it came to look us over, and got scared when we yelled. Is that why they took Marapese, just to see what he was like?"

"They're curious," Shari said. "That's why they took me. I was different from the others."

"Different?"

"Female."

"Oh."

In the quiet, there was a sudden feeling of activity. Clumps of reed shook where there was no wind. Things plopped and swirled in the water. Out of nowhere a small pink-and-mud-colored form appeared under Kirby's feet, tripped him, and flickered out like a picture when the film breaks. From then on the walk turned strange. The air was full of gurgles, grunts, and pleased little snortings, but the bodies that produced them moved so fast that they left the sounds eerily behind. Spouts of water flew up and drenched the two humans. Objects, twigs, berries, lots of mud, live fish, startled frog-like things,

137

pelted them out of the clear air. Kirby began to get mad.

"The young ones like to play," said Shari. "They never really hurt . . ."

She disappeared. Kirby shouted, and then the ground was pulled out from under him. There was a flash so brief he only sensed it, and he was up to his neck in water in the middle of a herd of great somnolent beasts, the adult espees wallowing comfortably in warmth and idleness, hardly bothering to notice him.

Shari appeared in a clump of reeds and beckoned to him. He began to swim, very gently so as not to startle the creatures, and a feeling of helpless and frightened wrath brought him almost to the verge of tears. These great half-witted brutes could, if they wanted to, transport him a hundred miles away in the bat of an eyelash, and there was nothing he could do about it.

They did not choose to, and he made the reeds without interference. Holding tight to Shari's hand lest she vanish again, he looked at the hippopotamoid forms and wondered, "How come Marapese didn't see them when he was here? How could he have avoided it?"

"They hid from him. I told you they were timid. Now they are more used to humans, and besides . have spent all these days teaching them not to fea us." She sighed wearily. "They are so stupid. The cannot read thoughts, or understand them. But made them *feel* that we are friends."

She shook her head in a kind of agony. "Ol Kirby, the knowledge that is locked up in those grea thick heads! If they understood only a fraction of they would be like gods. And how do they use their power? Look."

She pointed to where an adult lay on his side, half in water, half on a bank of warm mud. A heap of succulent grass flicked into being a few inches from his nose. He lay with his mouth open and the grasses crawled into it. Kirby got the feeling that the beast only bothered to chew them because the taste was pleasant.

"They can shift atoms," Shari said. "They can hold the unstable ones so that there is no emission of particles. In fact, they have complete mental control over matter, and they can do all these things singly or as a group with enormous potential. And in this way they feed themselves and repel their enemies and keep their wallows at just the right temperature, all without the slightest effort. It isn't fair! Men have labored so hard for thousands of years to learn just a little of what these creatures are born with but never understand!"

"I don't know," said Kirby. "Maybe our Mother Nature was smarter than this one. She made us work."

He sat for some time, watching the heap of fodder move obediently into the waiting mouth. When it was all gone the espee sighed a mighty sigh, rumbled twice, and rolled over on his back to sleep.

Kirby said, "They're not dangerous."

"No. Oh, in a panic they might do harm, more or less by accident. But not otherwise."

"Then the message from the R-ship was a lie."

"Yes. They hamper human activity as soon as it invades their forest, but the simple remedy for that to stay away and not bother them. They are completely lazy and unaggressive. Only a great stimulus of fear would cause them to use their power as far away as the *Lucy B. Davenport*. Of course, the people who sent that message may not know that it's untrue."

"I doubt if they care," said Kirby, "but I see what you mean. When RSS-1 orbited over this part of the forest the espees probably blanked off all the recording devices, among other things, so nothing showed up here at all. There may well be other swamps with other espees, too, and from the holes in the record and the signs of temporary malfunction in the operations of the ship the Government technicians would known there was something peculiar here, but not what it was."

He looked at his watch and then at the sky, and said, "So now we have the truth, and what good does it do us? The R-ship will land in approximately thirty minutes. We haven't a hope of getting back."

He stopped. Shari gave him a look of alarm.

"No!" she said. "They are uncontrollable, unpredictable. They—"

"They sent Marapese back, didn't they?"

"Pure chance. They could send us anywhere, and it might not be together."

"Listen," said Kirby. "The ship will land. The people will all get into it, and the ship will go away. Forever. Do you understand what that will mean for us?"

"But," said Shari, "I think—" She looked at the espees and moaned. "Intelligence one may bargain with, or reason with, or at the very least one may guess what the course of action may be. But with such imbeciles, who can say?"

Kirby pulled her to her feet. "We'll go back to the edge of the swamp, in the direction of the ship. It may give them the idea. I'll use the field radio. I may be able to get a message through to Fenner before they stop it, or they may 'port us within reach of the ship. Or both. Anyway, we can hardly be worse off. Come on."

She hesitated, still doubtful. Then she touched Kirby's arm and whispered, "Look."

The sleeping espee on the mudbank had waked again. He heaved himself over and raised his head as though to listen. A second or two later he snorted uneasily and was gone.

An expression of apprehension came into Shari's face. "Yes," she said. "We must go."

Out in the warm water the great bodies stirred and shifted, as if some sudden current had disturbed them. Then they, too, disappeared.

Shari began to move fast away from the water, through the reeds.

"What's the matter?" Kirby asked.

"They have caught the first vibrations from the R-ship."

"Oh, lord," said Kirby, and began to run.

They came out on a sunny bank. A shoal of the young espees, probably including the one Shari had held in her arms, lay snoring together in the mud, worn out by their frolic. Kirby asked, "How far did he little demons send us, anyway?"

"I don't know. Half a mile. More." She fled past he young ones. Kirby followed. They splashed hrough a slough and then Shari pointed back at he bank. Some of the small espees were already one. Others vanished while he watched, flick-flick-

flick. In no more than a second the bank was empty.

"They have gone back to the herd, where it has moved deeper into the swamp," said Shari. She plucked his sleeve. "Hurry!"

She had forgotten all about not running or making too much noise. It seemed that that no longer mattered. They hurried together through the swamp, and once again their passage acquired a strangeness. This time it was not the overt acts of the young ones. This was different. This was quiet, and tightening all the time until even the non-sensitive Kirby could feel each nerve stretched and singing like a fiddle string.

Finally he stopped of his own accord and listened. The silence ached in his ears. It was not merely a negation of sound. It was a force in itself, a positive thing. And there was something behind it. He felt it as a man feels the bulking potential of a tornado in the first capful of wind.

"They have gathered," Shari whispered. "They are all together now."

She rushed away again, with her hands on either side of her head. Her face was ashen. Kirby caught up with her. He stopped her and said, "We can't go any farther, there isn't time. We'll have to try it from here."

"No," she said. "No, Kirby, don't." She started to say something more, and then she crumpled down on the ground, all curled up and moaning. "Too close, too strong, I can't shut it out."

He got down beside her and pulled her up so that she was lying across his knees. She threw her arms around him tight and pressed her head in against his chest. Kirby's heart was pounding, fast and hard

He unslung the pack and opened it and fumbled out the radio.

Shari lifted her head. She screamed and grabbed for his wrist. He struck her hand away. The switch clicked. "Fenner! Fenner, this is Kirby. Don't—"

Static, a roar and a crash that split his ears. The radio flew out of his hands and smashed to bits against a tree. Shari screamed again. He caught hold of her, not so much to save her as to save himself. Then something hit him, something intangible, something mighty, as the earth hits a crashing ship.

He was rolling over and over on the prairie. There was dust in his mouth. He was still hanging on to Shari. He saw her dark hair fly as they tumbled, saw it grow dun-colored in the dust. They fell apart and stopped rolling and lay there, and after a while, without moving, Shari whispered, "I tried to warn you. They were afraid, and all together. They might have killed us."

"They weren't gentle," Kirby said, sitting up painfully. "But they were strong, all right. Too strong. Look."

Shari crawled to him. No more than a mile away the *Lucy B. Davenport* lay in the bright sunlight. They could see the people gathered near her, a dark blot on the lighter soil. They could see the pattern of the plowed land with the flush of green deepening on it from the sprouting crops, and they could see the sawmill and the streets that were going to be, with the square stone begnnings of the houses. Only a mile, but it might as well have been ten or a hundred, because the river was between them and three quarters of that mile was water.

And the R-ship was coming down.

They could see it, glittering in the high blue air, huge and cold and unconcerned, doing the thing it had been told to do. Inside its shining hull the innumerable relays clicked and whirred, the radar impulses telling the control centers the exact altitude and rate of fall, the control centers regulating the thrust of the landing jets, and farther in, deep in, sealed off in perfect safety but sending its spreading ganglia to every farthest section of the ship, the great electronic brain presided, overseeing every action, evaluating every bit of information transmitted to it by its sensory members, orienting the total effort of the ship toward the fulfillment of the code commands set up immovably on the master tapes, recorded inexorably on the master dials.

The shining robot sank, and the people waited beside the *Lucy B. Davenport*, the old ship about to be robbed of her final glory. And across the river Kirby watched and did nothing because there was nothing he could do.

Shari whispered, "Wait. Look there!"

The R-ships landing jets burst out in violent flame and thunder. It hovered uncertainly for as long as a man might draw two breaths before it started down again.

Kirby stiffened. He started to speak, but Shari's hand was tight on his arm and she had that far-off listening look he had come to know.

Again the RSS-2 halted in its downward flight, a silver bubble poised on a pillar of fire.

Shari said, "Now I understand."

"What is it?" Kirby said. "What's happening?"

"Watch."

The landing jets cut out abruptly. The thunde

144

stilled, and the trembling of the ground. The RSS-2 hung momentarily in mid-air, incredibly unsupported. Then it vanished.

Even at that distance Kirby could hear the cry that went up from the waiting crowd. It came thin and faint across the water, and Kirby echoed it, triumphantly.

But only for a moment. The RSS-2 was returning, relentlessly obedient to the commands it had crossed 4.3 light-years of space to obey.

"Even together," Shari said, "they cannot release enough energy to teleport so great a mass very far away."

The ship came down as it had before, on the howling jets. And this time they did not cut off.

Kirby said, "They can't stop it."

"Wait. Oh, if I could make you see it! They learned every atom of the controlling brain when the first R-ship passed over them, photographing. They repelled it. They would have tried to repel the *Lucy* the same way, but we did not pass over them."

"Fortunately," said Kirby, shivering at the thought.

"The landing was made before they quite realized we were here, and then they were trying to find another R-ship, not knowing there could be another kind. Now they are on familiar ground again, and I can see—"

She broke off, holding her head once more between her hands, but this time she was laughing in a sheer hysteria of excitement.

"It makes me dizzy. There is no perspective. The whole brain, the little transistors, the atoms, the electrons streaming, all are the same. The atoms

145

shift, some of them, and all the time they dance and spin. The electron streams are broken up, moving in a different way—and now the needles on the dials move too, and on the code tapes a layer of atoms less than a micron deep is stretched to make them blank. This time they know the right combination. Before they must have tried endless permutations to find the relay system that controls the order to go away. There! The tapes are blank, the circuits are closed off, and the master dial has moved to . . ."

The RSS-2 staggered, swooped down like a bird wounded in flight, and then, bathed in tremendous fires, it regained its balance and roared upward into the bright sky.

". . . return-to-base," finished Shari, on a note of anti-climax.

Kirby watched until the silver shape had dwindled to a speck, and then to nothing. Across the river the people watched too, stunned into silence. And in the distant swamp, Kirby knew, the espees were watching too, not with their eyes but with whatever nerve it was that measured for them the proximity of fear-things. Presently when the nerve ceased to twinge at all they would sigh and heave and 'port themselves back to their nice warmwallows, as unaware of what they had done as a great cat is unaware of the total physiological, emotional, and social consequences following after the single casual stroke of its paw that has just opened up a hunter's bowels. This playing with atoms was to them as instinctive and casual as the paw-stroke used for the same reason and of no greater significance.

Kirby began to laugh. There was something joy

ous about watching all man's misspent ingenuity going down to defeat before a herd of muddy morons
that didn't even have to try terribly hard.

"They took care of it," he said.

"The first one frightened them badly. They remembered."

"I guess they are our friends, then, even if they
don't know it."

Shari said, "They'll know it in time, if we behave
as we ought to.

Kirby looked across the river, at the streets that
would be finished and the houses that would be
built, and the crops that would be harvested after
all. Nobody would be going back now. And it was
doubtful if more R-ships would ever come. He put
his arms around Shari and held her close.

"Maybe your espees aren't so stupid at that," he
said. "It's wonderful just to be alive and at peace."

FRITZ LEIBER

06218	The Big Time $1.25
30301	Green Millennium $1.25
53330	Mindspider $1.50
76110	Ships to the Stars $1.50
79152	Swords Against Death $1.25
79173	Swords and Deviltry $1.50
79162	Swords Against Wizardry $1.25
79182	Swords in the Mist $1.25
79222	The Swords of Lankhmar $1.25
95146	You're All Alone 95¢

Available wherever paperbacks are sold or use this coupon.

Ursula K. Le Guin

10703	City of Illusion	$1.75
47803	Left Hand of Darkness	$1.95
66953	Planet of Exile	$1.25
73293	Rocannon's World	$1.50

Available wherever paperbacks are sold or use this coupon.

John Brunner

01000	Age of Miracles	95¢
03301	Atlantic Abomination	$1.25
05301	Bedlam Planet	$1.25
38121	The Jagged Orbit	$1.25
81271	Times Without Number	95¢
91051	The World Swappers	$1.25

Available wherever paperbacks are sold or use this coupon.

ACE SCIENCE FICTION SPECIALS

10150 Challenge The Hellmaker
Richmond $1.25

20660 Endless Voyage Bradley $1.25

21430 Equality in the Year 2000
Reyndds $1.50

25461 From the Legend of Biel
Staton $1.50

30420 Growing Up In the Tier 3000
Gotschalk $1.25

37171 The Invincible Lem $1.50

46850 Lady of the Bees Swann $1.25

66780 A Plague of All Cowards
Barton $1.50

71160 Red Tide Chapman & Tarzan
$1.25

81900 Tournament of Thorns
Swann $1.50
